Tales
from a
Greek Island

Roger Jinkinson

Copyright © Roger Jinkinson 2005

The right of Roger Jinkinson to be identified as the author of this work has been asserted by him in accordance with the Copyright, Designs and Patent Act 1988.

All rights reserved. No part of this work may be published or otherwise circulated in any form without the express permission of the publisher.

ISBN 1 84327 997 5

Cover design Patrick T. Coyne

First published in Great Britain 2005 by Racing House.

The Racing House Press
20 Cambridge Drive
London SE12 8AJ, UK

Printed and bound in the UK by Lightning Source

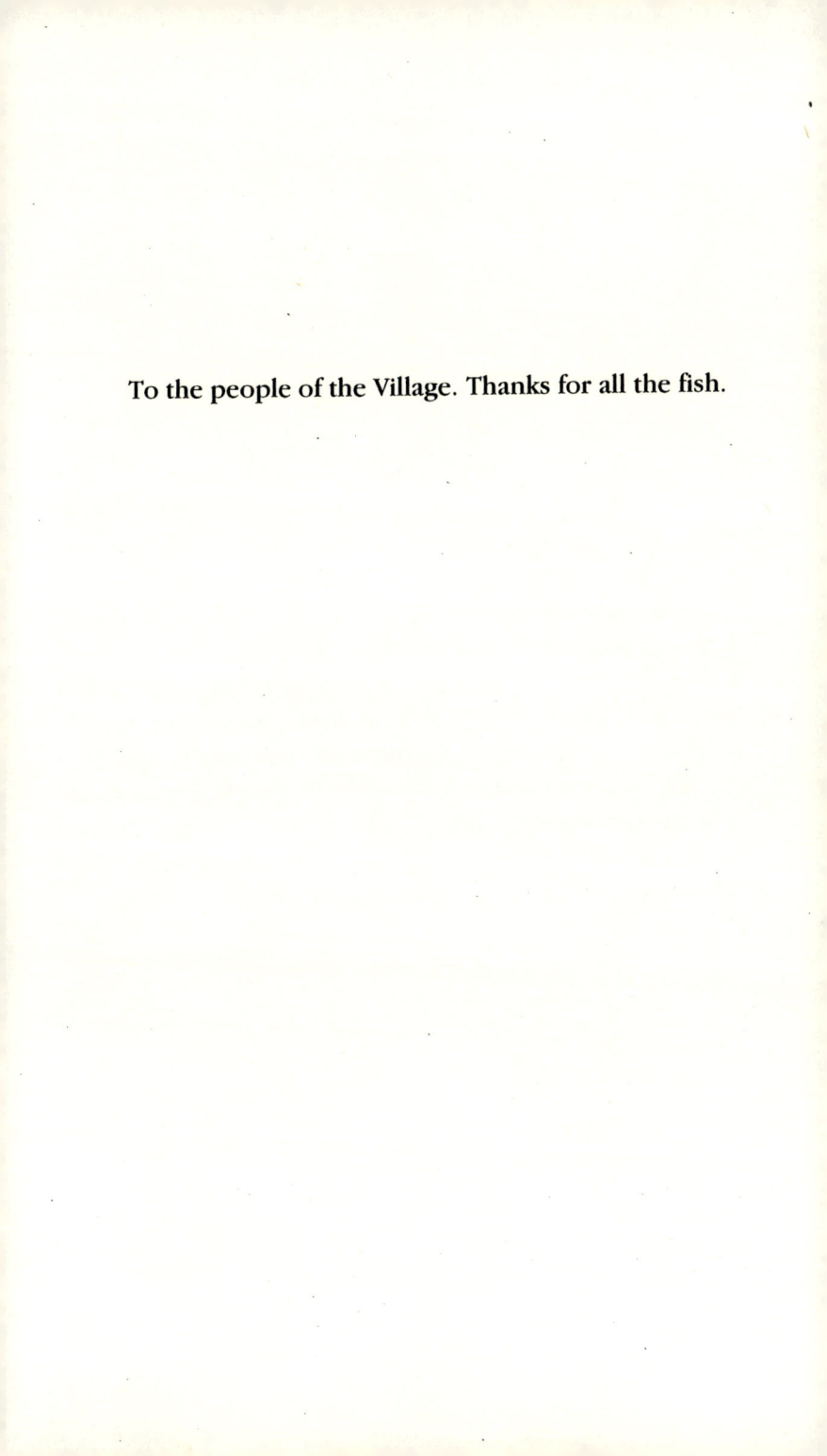

To the people of the Village. Thanks for all the fish.

Roger Jinkinson was born in the UK and has lived most of his life in London. Working in Higher Education, Roger's first job was cleaning the toilets. Later he became a lecturer and was appointed Deputy Vice Chancellor of a London University. After six years he quit to go fishing and spend more time among the people he loves. Roger first visited the Village in 1981 and over the years has come to appreciate and understand its values and traditions. Roger now has a house in the village and divides his time between fishing and diving, bee keeping, writing and photography. So far, he has resisted the many offers to keep goats.

Contents

To Live in Greece 1
Europe in the Twenty First Century 9
A Funny Looking Little Man...14
The Voyage..20
The Village 24
Kosmas...32
The Boots...40
The Gays 45
The Musician...48
The Golden Beach 52
Steno..55
John 61
Death in a Greek Village 72
The Lesson 81
Ballanos 89
Emetis from Embola 94
The Mule...98
Mosaic...104
The Woman at the Cemetery 111
How to Fish...119
Michaelis and the Crane 124
The Junta 132
The Mermaid and the Hunchback 136
We have Commandos here 150
The Story of the Cave..155
The Big Fish 159
Diaspora..167
The *Cafeneion* 171

To Live in Greece

To live in Greece is to be blessed; blessed by light, blessed by mauve mountains washed by fresh thyme in the early summer and blessed by a cool breeze in the early evening as you lie on warm stones by the sea and listen to children playing. To live in Greece is to understand history; to live daily with catharsis, tragedy, pathos and comedy. It is to be blessed and it is to be cursed; cursed by stubborn people, cursed by lies, delays, unexplained disappearances, unexpected arrivals. To live in Greece is to be cursed by oppressive heat and by the knowledge that the soil is soaked in blood. Greece is not confined by its boundaries; everyone who looks Greek, thinks Greek or speaks Greek is Greek. There are Greeks in Afghanistan and Mozambique, Australia and America. And yet when asked the people do not tell you they come from Greece. They say they come from this village or that island. Greece does not exist and yet it is everywhere.

To live in my village is to know secret corners; places I can visit, places no better, nor worse than anywhere else in the world, but little corners that distil my history and my feelings for life. Balconies, where I can sit as night falls and listen to soft voices from the village people as the sea grows black and the sky turns a unique blue before it too darkens and the stars spread themselves around. I can hear owls;

the Little owl that appeared on drachma coins in Athens 2500 years ago and Scops owl with its sharp notes; call return, call return, call return. There are windows here where I can sit and watch the church tower achieve its white silhouette against the night sky. There is a room where I lie at night and listen to the fishing boats come and go. That's Sortiris now, going north, and Costas too. Later it is Iannis with his overpowered outboard, or Karellas with an engine as clapped out as he is, in a boat kept together by thick, gaudy paint. In the morning I hear Michaelis with his dogs, his ninety year-old mother and his wife going to Saria. They will stay there for a week or two and they like fresh milk so they take goats with them in the boat. I could lie in bed all day and know the village from its sounds. In the morning there are cockerels, in the evening the sound of goats and sheep and all day dogs bark and children play. Then there are the voices of the women, their own private language low with chuckles and laughter round the oven as they bake bread, strong as they talk to a friend, or a sister, or a child further away. The tourist boat comes at its time and leaves with the flotsam and jetsam that is the European tourist trade; Danish, Dutch, German, Italian, a babble of barbarian voices and hysterical laughter. Now and then the ferry boat arrives, chains tumbling to the sea as the anchor seeks purchase against our strong winds. I hear the winds too. They play with my shutters; Trasmontana, Sirocco, Meltemi, Maestros. These names are ancient and Venetian; they remind us of what we were and tell us something of what we are. And then there is the sea, never silent, never still, the waves washing the stones in rhythms in the summer or pounding rocks when winter comes.

So this is Greece and this is my village. I want to introduce you to some of the people here and explain a little about our life. A fishing village in Greece is the dream of urban people everywhere, supposedly timeless and unchanged, as if these were desirable qualities. Maybe such places exist, but only in the barren dreams of people made impotent by the thirst for money, youth and success. We are not like that here. Maybe we are unique, but I feel that we are real, that we have found something about the possibility of living in harmony with a difficult landscape in a difficult world. I have tried to portray our community as it comes to terms with change and deals with the burden of history. Wherever possible I have tried to allow the people to speak for themselves. If there are mistakes in style, or in substance, then the mistakes are mine, for I am restricted in technique and running out of time

The visitors' perception of our village is limited. To them it is always hot and always sunny. The smarter ones recognise that it is nearly always windy too, but not much more. Those of us that live here have to be more observant. We have to travel by boat so we care if the wind is north or northwest, or even north northwest. We know it is often calmer in the morning than in the afternoon when the weather comes from the south and that, when it is from the north, there is often a lull around dusk. We inform our neighbours and ask for advice before we set off on a long journey by sea. We do this because our weather can change in half an hour and we know that if something goes wrong then someone from the village will look for us if they know where to look.

In the winter, if we are lucky, it will rain. If we are very lucky it will rain early and several times. Then we say that the rains are useful and we know that our crops will grow and there will be green across the island throughout the year. Two crops are particularly affected by rain: wheat and olives. In many years the winter rains are so poor that nobody plants wheat at all. A whole cycle of traditions are held in abeyance; the ploughing, the sowing, the reaping and the separating of the wheat from the chaff. Of course, the flour made from our own wheat and ground in our own windmills makes the bread baked in our ovens that much tastier. Each of the stages of growing and harvesting, processing and baking is accompanied by its own traditions, with its own songs and words. Many of these words and traditions are known only to the women and it is always with great pleasure that we see young girls learning from their mother, grandmother and sometimes, sitting in the shade of the oven, learning from their great grandmother too. Good winter rains bring us good harvests and at the same time our culture and our knowledge of the old ways springs up from the soil anew. If it rains in late October or early November we are especially pleased because the rain cleans the olives before we pick them and that makes life easier. Our olives are small and bitter, but they make fine olive oil and we produce soap too. Some olive trees have their own names. We know when they were planted and we know which of our forebears planted them and we talk to them as we pass by. When we had the big fire and the pine forests and olive groves burnt, we had problems with women who went into the fields clinging to loved trees that were doomed. We had to drag them screaming and weeping back to the village. We did not lose any women, but we did lose many olive trees. Over the years we have planted them again. A sign of renewal and hope and a wish for subsidies from the European Union.

Through the winter we are fearful of the Sirocco, the south wind that can do so much damage to our boats and even to the houses in the village. Many times we have sat in the cafe watching a storm when a big wave has come over the mole, over the beach and the road and dumped water, sand, stones and muck right among us. We lift up our feet as the water swirls under the benches and tables and then it subsides and Anna comes, waving her broom and shouting at us for being so stupid and at the sea for being so evil.

It doesn't take long to brush away the stones and at least the toilets get cleaned. Winter here can be cold; not every day, but for days on end. Our houses are cold too. Not many of the new ones have chimneys and concrete is not as good an insulator as limestone or slate. When the sun shines the women sit outside and the men fight in the *cafeneion* for the next sunny spot, otherwise doors are closed and the village too. Much work is done in the winter; building, carpentry and farming too, but there are not so many of us here to do the work. Much of the village is empty, as our children go to school, or to university, and their families follow them to the south of the island or to Rhodes or Piraeus, or maybe to the United States. Grand parents and great grand parents follow too and visit hospitals and old friends in far away places. I have never been to Baltimore, but it must be strange to the people there that Greek restaurants open in the winter and close in the summer so that their owners and their families can come here to swim and fish and have fun.

Springtime can be the best season. The sun starts to warm our backs in the fields as early as February and within a few weeks our fields and mountains are filled with flowers; green leaves appear and herbs as well. There are red poppies and white neragoula and narcissi too and those of us who walk in the forests marvel at the tiny bee orchid, its flowers mimicking the bumblebee to attract pollinators. Migrant birds appear; the small passerines, bee-eaters and rollers, hoopoes and birds of prey. From the cliff tops it is possible to see eagles pass by; beating a passage over the sea, heading north against the wind, flying close to the waves to give them lift. Booted eagles, short toed eagles, golden eagles come to join our resident Bonelli's. We see black kites and long-legged buzzards and once, huge and beautiful, an eagle owl heading north to the Russian steppes. Cuckoos pass by and swallows, swifts, alpine and pallid, and then we wait for the first tourists. These always catch us by surprise. The rooms have not been cleaned since October, the sheets are not washed, we have only half painted the house and of course the rubbish brought by the winter storms has not been cleared from the beach. But we are glad to see tourists; they bring laughter and fun and sit in our cafe and our restaurants and we renew old friendships and start new ones. Springtime is a season of change for us.

By mid May the last Sirocco has ceased to blow and the summer wind, the Meltemi, is blowing strong from the north. The artichokes are ripe by now and the beehives double in population every week or two. But it can be hot, far too hot. So we work in the early morning, when the sun is not strong and the tourists still asleep and the women bake bread at five in the morning and their low voices mix with wood smoke as we sleep on roofs and balconies.

The summer wind is always from the north and it never rains, but you will not see us working in the fields. There is some activity however on the mountains around Avlona or in Saria, as bee hives are moved to catch the thyme as it blooms. A good season will bring reward and in this part of the island more than ten tonnes of honey is produced and tourists can buy the real thing rather than the cheaper varieties imported from Crete, or Denmark, or China. In the *cafeneion* Anna will advise on the coolest place to sit and where to catch a cooling breeze. But by August there is no room for any of us in the *cafeneion* as the village is full of visitors; Italians and French and Germans too, as well as our own people returned from exile. So the hotels are full and most of the houses are occupied and doors and windows that have been closed for months, or even years, are open once again. Lights are on at night all over the village and there is a smell of mothballs and sun tan lotion. Guitars are played on the beach until the early morning and it could be anywhere but here. So the people, who come for something unique, find only something recognisable all over the world — a holiday atmosphere. Perhaps they are satisfied.

No matter, this time passes quickly and by the middle of September the crowds have gone and the restaurant owners are pleased to see you and we can go diving without being followed by a flotilla of Italians hoping for us to lead them to the big fish. And now there are kingfishers, a pair on each bay, speeding back and forth exactly half a metre above the sea. They sit on rocks and dive, neatly to seize *atherinos*, the little fish that cling to our shores in late summer. Where kingfishers come from and where they go I do not know. I have asked ornithologists and they cannot tell me. I have never seen a nest, but I think they breed here, late, in the rocks and in the cliffs. Soon they are gone too and the passerines pass by at night, hunted and harried by Eleanora's falcons as they hug the coast heading for Africa. The swallows head south in late September and October and then the eagles and falcons arrive in Saria and seek ever more powerful thermals. They go higher and higher until they can see the weather to Crete and even Africa and then they are gone. Herons and egrets stay for a while, then one late evening, or on a bright night, we see the silhouettes of skeins of birds going south and summer is gone.

We are back to autumn again and peace in the village, but the olives need to be picked and crops planted and there are ripe figs to be gathered and so much fruit. We need to fish to fill the freezers, for the winter storms will come again from the south and deprive us of sea bream and silver bream and red and grey mullet, *palamida* and tuna. And of course we must fix that room and paint the house to be ready for next season.

As for me, the time I like best is the onset of winter. Sometimes, when the rains come, it is still warm enough to sit on my balcony at night, in the dark and listen to the drops singing on the roofs outside and smell the freshness of the pine forest, a glass of whisky in my hand and a head full of memories. Or it can be cold and windy and then it's time to go to Anna's and squeeze through the door and sit inside and watch the men playing cards, or *tavli*. An ouzo is called for now and I listen to the shouts of the men and the storm outside and watch moisture trickle down a windowpane. Then I know that I am really in the first chapter of a fine novel by Kazantzakis and I am glad.

Europe in the Twenty First Century

Living in a small village may seem idyllic and sometimes it is, but it can also be difficult. To start with, everyone knows you and knows your business. There is nothing sinister about this. You live in a small space and you see the same faces several times a day. So you ask them how they are and where they are going and can you help them carry this load, or catch that goat? There are feuds going on all over the place, some of them generations old, but normally we all get on well. However, sometimes life is too hectic. Maybe someone steals someone else's tourist, or leaves rubbish in the street and a fight starts. Or maybe an election is on its way and the threat of democracy tears at the fabric of the village. Then it is time to leave, to go away somewhere quiet, to be alone, to reflect gently on life. I needed such a day. The village had been getting to me. I would go to Tristomo. This is a magic place, a long lagoon, like the footprint of God, the other side of the island. There is a village, deserted except for Iannis and his wife who lead tranquil lives. They have sheep there and bees, they gather wild herbs and fruit and vegetables, they garden and they take their pick of the flotsam that arrives by the hour from the civilised world. Iannis is sixty-five and immensely strong, his wife has the same age and they live without electricity, or toilet, or running water. There are no roads, no shops, no cars, just the sea and the mountains and the wind singing through ruined houses. There are memories in Tristomo. Maybe, there are ghosts.

I would go there, reflect, have a quiet day by myself. I would have to pass through the dangerous straits at Steno, but never mind, the sea was calm. I would fish and take photographs. I went to my boat. I didn't have enough petrol and there was none in the shop. I asked around; Michaely, Maki, Gabriella. No joy. But Georgos had some! Poor Georgos has a broken foot so can't get his wet suit on. He can't dive.

I will come with you and sit in the boat while you take pictures. He tells me.

Not what I wanted, but it was his petrol. So. . . . When we get to the boat Nick is waiting there with a big, black bag.

He wants to come too. Nick is a nice guy, a good friend. He's a bit wild, but he wants to come too. Could I say no? We got Georgos into the boat then the bag and then Nick. We set off.

Immediately the two of them start arguing. Lots of *malakas* (wanker) and you know nothing, mixed with I taught you everything you know. After five minutes I explain. This is my boat; I am the captain and the owner. I want a quiet day, so shut fucking up.

They shut fucking up.

For two minutes. Peace, silence, calm sea, sunlight, dappled waves.

It is when Nick opens the black bag, takes out a rifle and starts to clean it, that I realise the day is not going to go exactly as I had planned.

The first thing he wants to shoot is a cormorant.

Not in my boat.

Why not?

It's a nice bird.

It's a duck.

It is not a duck.

It's tasty.

No, fucking way.

The ecologist wins, but having eaten pigeon, I can't really object to a few for the pot. The pigeons do. They fly very fast. Nick misses. One up to the pigeons.

We arrive at Tristomo. I get out and wander round the village for a couple of hours. I peer into the old houses, climb collapsed walls, take some pictures, but do not have any *kefi*, or feeling for this work. Three men in a boat is two too many. I take some bad pictures. I lie on a wall. I doze in the sun. Feel better. Feel relaxed.

Into my field of view I can see Georgos in the water; stark naked, swimming slowly along. A few feet behind, rowing my boat and discretely looking the other way, comes Nick. Surprisingly, Greek men are very prudish. Georgos and I have often stripped off in my little boat, to change into our wet suits and I have never seen, well, you know what I have never seen. Neither has Nick and he clearly doesn't want to, so he looks the other way. Every so often, Georgos dives down a few feet under the water, leaving his still bandaged foot waving in the air and surfaces with a large octopus in his hand. Without looking he throws this over his shoulder. Nick catches the octopus, smashes it with a piece of wood and puts it in a plastic bag. All this in total silence. Alice in a Greek Wonderland.

They come closer. Georgos gets into the boat. We look the other way as he dries on a handkerchief and gets dressed.

We fish for a while with nets, to catch the tiny, tasty fish, *atherinos*; like whitebait, but a little larger. We catch a few kilos. As the others clean the nets I steer the boat and pull the lure. I catch *kinygos*, Dolphin fish. These are big fish, more then two kilos. Nice fish. Tasty fish. I am excited as we pass through the straits of Steno. I had seen a golden eagle the day before, and a marsh harrier. I swap places with Georgos and I sit with my binoculars expectantly.

Look, I say, *agrimi* (wild goats) and know immediately I have made a mistake. Within seconds Nick is standing on the front of the boat, waving his gun and shouting *malakas* at Georgos as he puts cartridges into his pocket. We land him on the rocks and off he goes, fast up the cliff, bent low, ponytail waving, rifle in his outstretched arm. Geronimo. He makes his way up hill, up wind. We look furtively around. They are called wild goats, but someone must own them. We see no speedboats, no fishing boats, no port police.

Crack, crack.

Two hits. One goat down, the other limping.

Malakas. From Georgos.

Who is *malakas*?

You missed. *Malakas*.

I am not *malakas*. You are *malakas*.

This style of conversation is commonplace in Greece.

Nick comes slowly down the cliff, rifle in hand, picks up the dead goat. Carrying it over his shoulder he stalks the other one, now close to the water line. Suddenly he throws the dead goat into the water.

Grab it, says Georgos. Take its horns. Pull into the boat.

I do as I am told, but it's not easy to pull a dead, wet goat out of the sea. I manage. Blood, foam, guts. Then, as Nick takes aim, the wounded goat tumbles into the sea by itself.

Grab it.

I grab it. It floats listlessly, head under water, feet moving. It is still alive.

Kill it.

The poor creature is in difficulties. I take a knife and start sawing at its throat. There is blood in the water. I look around for the port police. I see the headlines. Englishman caught sheep stealing. I see my picture in the paper. Will I be sent to Australia? Nick comes down the cliff, gun held high. He jumps into the boat, takes the knife from my weak hand and finishes off the job. This is a large goat, it takes the two of us to pull it out of the sea.

We look around. Blood, foam, shit, silence. No port police.

We change places. Now I am captain again. I take the tiller, I drag the lure. We continue on our way. We head for home in the twilight, a smidgeon of moon, a calm sea. No boats. No watching eyes. Only *Aphrodite* (Venus) twinkles above the hillside.

For some days I have been wondering why such a large piece of wood has appeared in my boat. For sure it is handy for dispatching large fish, or an octopus, but we have other means. Why am I so naive? As well as carpenter, fisherman, musician, Georgos is a butcher. This is a butchers' block. The pair of them start to cut up the dead beasts. It is an efficient job. Black bags appear, heads and feet (a local delicacy) in one, lights and liver (ditto) in another. Skins are punctured and sunk. Intestines are emptied, turned inside out and washed (Nice when barbecued. No, really.). Blood and shit is washed from the boat, blood washed off the ropes. Knives are washed, the gun dismantled and we are home. The two of them disappear into the dark, loaded down with black sacks.

I anchor the boat. Go home. Shower. Go to the *cafeneion*. I need a whisky. I have an ouzo, then another and another. I sit outside, quietly in the shadows, listening to Anna as she tells the men what the weather will be like tomorrow. Ah, tomorrow. Perhaps a quiet day. If I could go to. . . No, it's better to stay in bed.

A Funny Looking Little Man

If you stay in the village for more than a few days you are bound to notice a funny looking little man. Well the truth is that you will notice more than one, but I am referring to one in particular. His name is Minas and he is the father of my friend Georgos.

My father is a very strange system, says Georgos and it is true. A very strange system indeed.

Minas is a carpenter, or was a carpenter, one can never be sure. He is retired, but he works, mainly for the church. He fixes things, does those fiddly little things that nobody else wants to do. A window frame replaced here, a new lock fitted there. Minas is a careful worker, he does not like to see things thrown away. Round the village you will notice old chairs, or benches, or stools with new bits grafted onto them; half a leg maybe or a new back. A bit of glue, a few nails and a lowly piece of hand made furniture will last another decade. He has worked in the village for over fifty years now. His handiwork can be seen in the *cafeneion*, in the church hall, in the little yard outside his house. When he is gone his work will live on around us. We will remember him as we sit on a wooden bench or place our coffee on a simple, weathered table.

Minas is a charming man and very smart. In his youth he was very handsome, the village Romeo, and is still a great musician. Minas is truly a *meraklese,* a musician who can make things happen at festivities. I am proud that I know his style and when I hear *da detheda da detheda da* coming from the church hall on some name day festivity I can recognise it is Minas playing and know that, as we say, he is flying with the seagulls. When I go inside he will be sitting there with the others, on a little stool placed carefully on a big table, lyre buzzing, feet tapping in that strange medieval beat, his thick glasses slipping from the end of his nose. He will nod to me and smile and I will sit below him, push his glasses back to the top of his nose and hold a whisky to his lips. We will drink from the same glass and the music will not stop. *Da detheda da detheda da detheda da.*

During the time of the Junta, Yannis Markopoulos, one of the leading traditional musicians of Greece, was exiled to the most distant and remote village the colonels could find. They sent him here. Markopoulos was expected to crack up under the loneliness and isolation. Instead he discovered Minas and recognised his genius. They became friends and played music every day. Indeed when Markopoulos was allowed to travel again he asked Minas to tour with him, to be a star. But modest Minas said no and stayed in the village. His artistry is not unrecognised; the older people respect him as a great musician and even the young people collect his tapes and gather round and listen with awe as they try to capture his style.

Tragedy has struck twice in this man's life, but you have to find this from others not from him. The first blow was when his first wife died, less than a month into the marriage. I know no more than that, but it explains some of his behaviour and why he is such a deeply private, sensitive and pessimistic man. The second came later. Still a young man and at the height of his musical powers Minas had a close friend and musical partner, Yannis Tzerkis, a lute player. The pair were great friends and partners and, as only Greeks can be, were totally inseparable. They played music every day, went everywhere together and were famous throughout the island. They played at festivals, weddings, baptisms, everywhere. They made tapes together and even a little money. Then Yannis died in a building accident. He fell from a roof and Minas put down the lyre and did not have the *kefi* to pick it up again for ten years. So there is reserve to his love. It is not given easily.

Minas is now married to Marina, my adopted mother. Many of the women in the village are big. They work hard, they eat well and as they get older they grow. Some are enormous. Marina is one of those. Her several layers of clothes make her look bigger still and as she walks along with her five and a half feet husband Marina seems two or three times his size. She nags and scolds him too, referring only to his surname. Prearis does this, Prearis does that. He is useless, he is lazy, he is always complaining. The latter is true, the rest is part of the daily theatre of village life. She scolds Minas and reaches into the many pockets hidden in her skirts and hands out sweets to children and delicious bread and cookies to passers by. He walks silently alongside, chewing his toothless gums and raising his hands and eyebrows in supplication to seek support from any man that passes by. The villagers are used to this and ignore the performance. Neither do they say anything about the daily shouting matches that come from the little house, half way up the hill in that part of the village known as Gimonas. Winter. In fact the only comment I have heard about this behaviour was from a friend of mine, one of their neighbours. She told me that early one morning she heard the voice of Marina, soft and loving.

Come on my darling, come on my little love. Come here my little dear.

So strange was this that she got out of bed to peek at this unexpected display of love and affection. . . . and saw Marina feeding her chickens.

I love Minas very much. For some reason I find his constant complaints about his health and the prices in the *cafeneion* incredibly amusing. But it is always dangerous to ask him how he is, for he is never well.

Iassu Minas.

Ti Kaneis

Not good

Why not?

My knee hurts. And my ankle too.

Oh that's terrible. But you look well.

My varicose veins are painful and I have rheumatism. Oh, and down here (pointing to his crotch) there is nothing.

Nothing?

Nothing. For twenty years, nothing. Down there it is winter. When I was young my clock was at five past twelve, now the hands point to half past six.

And he laughs.

Me too.

Minas has a position in the church. Exactly what his title is I cannot say, but it is something to do with money. On Big Saturday, for example, the day before Easter Sunday, before Christ is declared to have risen, we crowd into the back of the church and push forward against the more pious villagers who have been there longer. Minas is at the back, by the door, lighting candles, passing them round, collecting money, not offering change. He is proud of the church. He loves the paintings, the icons that cover the walls from floor to cupola; dark, vibrant, frightening, primitive pictures completed by one of our own just a few years ago. In the gloom, if you take your time, you will see fishers of men, devils and sea monsters, angels and bats and strange saints, long forgotten in the west. You will recognise the illustrations of parables and Adam and Eve and St George slaying his own, individual, dragon. You can imagine that this work took a long time and it had to be paid for, because even artists have to eat, but the method of payment was new to me.

I was sitting quietly outside in the little courtyard of Anna's. It was a late September evening, warm and calm with a large moon visible through the tamarisks. I was on my second ouzo and feeling content. Minas was sitting opposite me.

We like you, he said, for no obvious reason. We do not think of you as a tourist.

I am pleased with this. I thank him for his words.

We think of you as *horianos*, a villager. You are one of us.

Thank you. That makes me very happy.

No, it's true.

I feel deeply, deeply proud.

Thank you.

So why don't you pay for one of the icons in the church?

I pause. I hold my breath. I am trapped. I can't get out of it. He has me.

How much?

Well the big ones are . . .

No, no, I only want a little one.

Fifty thousand drachmas.

And that's it. I am going to donate fifty thousand to the church.

The next day we go round to chose a suitable painting. As we look I notice, for the first time, that many of the pictures have names of donors in their bottom right hand corner. The more prominent the picture, the more prominent the family that had made the donation. I recognise the names Orfanos and Balaskas, Protopapas and Papavassilis.

We look for a while, but all the saints are taken and anyway they are too big for me, too expensive. We peer about in the dark.

Up there that's a good one. At the top, just to the right. That's for you.

For me? Are you sure? What's its name?

I don't know. I haven't got my glasses on, but it's a hermit. It's for you.

I strain to see. It does look like a hermit, kind of lonely and ragged and wild, but a kind man and I don't think it has a signature.

So I bought a hermit. And now in the cupola, high up, just to the right, you will see my name low down in the corner of the picture of a strange looking man whose name I do not know. At least I think it is my name. It's too high up to see and I hate to think I am like one of those tourists who bought the Eiffel tower or the Brooklyn Bridge.

I stand there now, in the church, in the dark, looking up. I think of my *meraklese* and sigh as I turn away. I walk home up the steps to my little house. I hear his rhythm. *Da detheda da detheda da detheda da.* I see his chops chewing away, his slow walk, the thick glasses on the end of his nose. I think of the hands of his little clock perpetually stuck at half past six.

A strange system. A very strange system. And a lovely man.

The Voyage

I cannot believe I am doing this. I am in a little boat, four metres thirty, the sea is wild and I have twenty thousand passengers. I look to see if they are OK. I look in through the mesh, they look out. They seem OK, but then they can't see what I can; the waves, the rocks, the spray. An English sailor would call this sea lumpy, a Greek, with equal understatement, would say *ekei thalassa,* there is sea.

Thank God it is not windy. Waves can cause problems, they can break over your boat, especially if you go into them too fast, or you are too slow and a following sea catches you, but they do not drive you into the cliffs and onto the rocks. The wind does that and there is no wind, so I can keep in close to the cliffs, maybe five metres, and I can dodge in and out of the rocks. This close to the shore the waves are not so big. They break up as they rebound and meet the oncoming wave and create a choppy, lumpy, environment. Not dangerous, unless I make a mistake, but stressful and tiring and I have been up since four this morning.

I cannot believe I am doing this. Moving my beehive from the winter location, snug on a steep hill in the forest, to their own private valley by the sea in the north of Saria, the next island. There they will be ready for the blooming of *thymari*, the thyme, which, in two weeks will cover the mountains with a mauve wash and provide nectar and pollen and enable my lovely, lovely bees to flourish and give me honey. I was in the trees before dawn and it was dark and I had to approach the hive without light. I did not want to disturb the bees and have them come pouring out as I closed their entrance. They guard the entrance valiantly against robbers in daylight. But they were asleep inside as I approached and I had no problems. They were quiet too as I carried the hive down the mountainside, loaded it onto a truck and drove it to the beach. There they rested while I drank tea and waited for dawn.

It is best to transport bees in the cool of the night, so they do not suffocate, but the way to Saria is rough and in the dark that can be difficult, so we wait for the light. Bees regulate the temperature of their hive. If it is too hot they stand by the entrance and by the mesh and whirl their wings to circulate air. Too cold and they block up the mesh and the cracks in the wood with *propolis*, a magic, supposed healthy element, secreted by special glands. They make honey by collecting nectar, mixing it with water, storing it in the comb, whose cells slant slightly upwards to avoid drips. Then they cure the mixture, by maintaining the temperature precisely and evaporating off excess water. You and I make wine or beer in a similar way. We read books about it, we learn from our friends. But a bee? This tiny, furry creature. How does she know, for it's the females who do the work? How does she know what the temperature is and what to do about it? When the honey is ready, they cap it with wax, secreted by another gland, so that they can store it for the winter. As it happens, capping the comb means that I can transport full combs home without spilling any. We work together my bees and I.

As the sky grew lighter in the east I returned to the beach. I look through the mesh again. All is quiet; the workers are calm and deep inside, the queen is at ease. I have been taught to respect the queen. I do not call her *mana*, or mum, as the locals do. I am a beginner. A subject. To me she is *E Vassilissa,* the Queen. I loaded my twenty thousand passengers and the queen into my little boat and off we go in what looks to be a dead, calm sea. But not for long.

On my own I would turn back. It is too rough now, too difficult. I have to look in four directions at once, avoid this wave, slow down for that, wait behind this rock, then glide between those two small ones. And what's it going to be like in Alona? But when we reach Alona it is dead calm, dead flat. Sheltered from the Sirocco, the south west sea, it causes me, for the first time ever, no problems at all. Around the Mediterranean, wherever they grew wheat or barley, you will find in the old historic countryside round flat stone constructions among the terraces and the olive groves by the sea. In Greece, in the villages, they are called Alona. This is where they took advantage of the summer wind, the Meltemi, shaking the grain from the sheaf, breaking it a little then throwing the mixture up in the air so that the wind can separate the wheat from the chaff. If you have seen this you are lucky. If you read about it, then, no doubt, you will have been told it is biblical. It is not. They were doing this long before the bible became the confused oral history of tribes of nomads and farmers. So I cross the bay of Alona, away from the cliffs, away from the rocks. And Steno too is calm. The narrow, normally wild passage that separates Karpathos from Saria is benign today, the sea oily and flat like yoghurt.

I chug up the east coast of Saria as fast as I dare. The sun is climbing, the day warmer now. I don't want my bees distressed. They are by the mesh now in their hundreds, wings whirling, facing the breeze, keeping the hive cool, keeping alive. Me too. Still alive. Where are those rocks outside

Palatia? There. OK. Wide berth and we are at Alimounda, the summer residence. I anchor the boat, tie up on the beach, carry my little darlings two hundred metres inland. I place the hive in its spot, sheltered from the wind and the afternoon sun, and provide them with a little runway; for they like to land a few centimetres from the entrance to the hive and wait before walking in the entrance.

It is hot. I am tired. I rest for ten minutes. I put on my gloves, my beekeeper's mask and jacket. I light the smoker. It is the smell of smoke that enables us to work bees. They think there is a forest fire coming and they start to gorge on their honey, ready to transport it to a place of safety. I open the entrance, smoke it a little with the smoker and wait. Nothing. They do not come pouring out, an angry, dangerous, mass of high pitched buzzing. I have done my job properly. They are not frightened, they are calm. I walk away and sit quietly. A little while and a few bees come out to search for water, pollen and nectar. When they return they will perform a dance, a circle or figure of eight in front of the entrance to show the others what they have found and how far away and in what direction. They will be happy. Her majesty will be happy. Here there is plenty. I have done my job. Now they can do theirs.

The Village

I suppose it is best to start at the beginning, but I cannot. We do not know when was the beginning. For sure the Dorians were here and before them the Minoans, but I like to think that we were here before them. Certainly the first people to reach Karpathos were not farmers, not settled people with large families, but hunters and gatherers, moving from place to place in small groups, understanding the environment, keeping an eye on the weather, reading the wind, watching the sea. This has always been a green island with water and trees and there was plenty of fish in those days and shellfish too. There are many caves for shelter here. Most are unexplored, but if you go to the big ones and dig, then you will find bones and shells and seeds and charcoal from ancient fires. These are messages from our forebears, clues as to how they lived. You can see, near some of our beaches, piles of shells, exposed by the sea. Here, these early people would sit and eat, lie in the shade, swim perhaps, sleep in caves. The life of a hunter and gatherer would not be that difficult on an island like this. We have partridges and hares to hunt, wild asparagus, wild broccoli, capers, herbs, figs and cactus fruits to pick. From the sea, even without nets, even without simple boats, you can catch fish.

I could take you today to see places on the coast where half a dozen men could drive fish inshore. Using baskets, branches and sticks they would drive fish into a small enclosure, fill the entrance with rocks and they would have enough food for weeks. In those days the fish were plentiful and man could swim and dive to catch lobsters and crayfish, so rich in protein that we still think of them as a delicacy.

In early times, people came from the north, using the Meltemi to come south in the springtime, waiting for the weather to change in autumn and going back north with the Sirocco as the winter came. They would island hop, like the tourists do. Rhodes, large and forested, attracted them from what is known today as Turkey and they stayed for a few generations. Then they moved on to Halki, Saria and Karpathos. Each year they would travel back north in primitive boats laden with food for the winter. A few generations more and they stayed, lost contact with the north and settled in caves, forest shelters and simple huts. Were these the forefathers of today's people? Or were they pushed into the sea by farmers with new technologies and a desire to change the environment; people who came to slash and burn, importing seeds, planting fruit, bringing with them goats and sheep?

Maybe the farmers were the first ones with the oval eyes, the oval eyes that you see in paintings and frescoes in Minoan palaces. Go into any *cafeneion* here, look at the old photographs on the wall, black and white photographs taken fifty or sixty years ago. Teachers and school children, or priest and congregation stare obediently at this new machine. You will see dozens of identical pairs of eyes, looking out at you in total uniformity. Put down your drink. Look round the room. The same faces. The same eyes. Nothing has changed. They are the same people with the same eyes for more than 10,000 years. The ancient Greek word for round eyes was *evropoi*, in today's language, European. If you come from Denmark, or Germany, or the north, you are a round eye. The people from our village are not round eyes. Do you feel a little strange?

So the farmers came and others too. Homer wrote about us in the *Iliad* and we appeared on maps. The Minoans found that inland, surrounded by mountains, was a plateau with rich soil and plenty of water and they farmed there and built paved tracks to their beloved sea. Some of these tracks are with us still. At least half a dozen donkey tracks lead up and down to Avlona and are used now, as then, to transfer grain and vegetables and people and olives and that most precious commodity, dung.

The volcanic catastrophe at Santorini, three and a half millennia ago, blew half that island into the sky and destroyed the Minoan civilisation. The huge explosion and the tidal waves that followed were devastating enough, but the cloud of ash that covered the fields and hung in the atmosphere for seasons after, and the salinisation of fertile lands by the waves, meant that crops failed and Crete and the other islands could no longer support the Minoan superstructure. So people starved or they migrated and the population declined. In our part of the island they knew that Avlona was higher than any tsunami and they felt safe. They lived there for a while and then, as time passed, moved back to the sea. At Vrakounda and at Palatia in Saria they left their dead, the Minoan way, high up in caves in the surrounding cliffs.

If you go to Vrakounda now you will see walls made of large, sawn boulders, quarried from the ancient and spectacular landscape around you. These were built by the Dorians, descendants of the Minoans and a people skilled in engineering, but lacking the finesse of their ancestors. Perhaps you may not notice the most significant construction. It is too big to see. Look again. Carefully now. Look at the harbour. It is man made. Where Nikos ties up his boat or where you sit to have your picnic is a man made harbour. Those great twenty or thirty ton boulders did not fall in a straight line into the sea. They were cut by saw and drilled and split by fire and water, then, by mule and man with lever and fulcrum and maybe by oar and sail too, the shaped boulders were moved along into the sea and fitted together to provide shelter from the westerly wind.

Imagine the organisation required to drag hundreds of tons of rocks into position and you will get a feel for the size of the population that lived here. Then look around at the hillsides and you will understand why they needed all those terraces to grow food for this large population. Close your eyes and the hills and mountainsides will come alive with the sound of digging, of hoes hitting rocks and women calling to their children as dusk falls and the people move down the valley to their little town by the sea. The Dorians did not only leave behind these walls and rocks. They also left their language. Many of our words and much of the structure of our language is Dorian, not Greek. We can talk together so that sophisticated Greeks from the mainland cannot understand us. This is sometimes useful.

Karpathos acts as a stepping-stone between the mainland and Asia Minor. The natural harbour of Tristomo provided shelter in southerly winter storms and the east coast provides shelter from the more predictable summer Meltemi. The Greeks passed by; some settled and brought marble from Rhodes and built a temple to Poseidon, the god of the sea. Its exact location is unknown, but where better than Steno, the channel between Karpathos and Saria. Go there on a winters day, or in a summer storm and you will understand that you would want the god of the sea to look over you as you rowed or sailed through those narrow straits over razor rocks and fought the wind and the waves and the current that changes direction twice a day.

Poseidon was sometimes a wrathful god and those of us that dive know of ships that were sunk from the times of the Greeks. On the seabed we know where there are amphora and round stones used as ballast in old Greek vessels. They lie there still in the ghostly outline of a ship. The columns from the temple of Poseidon have been recycled more than once and you can see them in the churches and old buildings of Diafani, Palatia, Tristomo, Vrakounda and Olymbos.

Perhaps Alexander the Great was here too. Maybe Vrakounda and Tristomo were used as ports as he transported his armies to Asia Minor? I have no evidence for this, except that there are old people who think it true and there are families from Tristomo and from Saria who have piercing blue eyes. I have seen these same eyes in Afghanistan and was told that those people were descended from the Macedonians of Alexander. If Afghanistan, why not Saria?

Tristomo and Vrakounda were the most important settlements in the north well into the first millennia. The people there were not mere farmers, but civilised, educated people. The Dorian decree, an inscribed marble plaque from the 3rd century BC, found in Tristomo, but unfortunately now in the British Museum, reads as follows:

> Menokritos, a doctor, practised in Vrykus for 20 years now, has lived in poverty and has not demanded a drachma. Out of human kindness he has helped the sick and also guests from abroad who he did not know. Neither has he avoided the paths to remote hamlets in order to offer his skills and assistance free of charge. For the sake of this service to mankind, it now pleases the people of Vrykus to honour Menokritos with a golden crown and to have it made publicly known and to proclaim his fame far and wide, during the Aeskulapian plays. Further the crown is to

be paid for out of the town's funds and a plaque erected in the Poseidon Porthmios temple.

We do not treat our young doctors so well these days, but we are pleased to have them.

The Romans were here, but left little to show for the distance they travelled. Christians passed through and there are sarcophagi in Vrakounda as proof and stories of saints and monks. Also scattered about, but normally close to the sea, are remains of churches and basilica. Some of these have large foundations that show evidence of their importance and the size of the population required to fund their construction.

From around the 6th to 13th centuries marauders, or pirates, surged over the island and settled in Saria at Palatia. The local people moved inland to Olymbos, fortified and safe and unpainted, so as not to attract attention from the sea. In the following centuries the external rulers changed; Turks from Byzantium, the Knights of St John from Rhodes, Venetians, Russians and once again the Turks. But the people did not change and there is little evidence of their occupiers. Only the Venetians left their mark. If you walk along the valley to Olymbos from Diafani or walk inland from Vananda you will see water channels cut in the rocks and even one or two water chutes and the remains of simple water mills.

In the nineteenth and twentieth centuries the great powers intervened, dividing up Greece and ignoring its right to independence. The Turks were forced out in 1912 to be replaced by the Italians, but neither made much impression up here in the north. The Turks collected taxes, but ruled with a light touch and visited Olymbos and Diafani rarely. There are old people alive who still remember them, with their baggy trousers, and some words remain in our language. The Italians meddled more and stationed their military here, as well as tax collectors and bureaucrats, but in the main they are well thought of and there was even some mingling of the blood and the occasional marriage. Several of the old people speak Italian and many of the words we use at sea such as *bonnatsa* (calm) and *prima* (following wind) are Italian, if not Venetian, in origin. Life became more difficult when Italy invaded the Greek mainland, but the leaders here decided to resist the enemy passively rather than take up arms. Many of the men slipped away to fight and there was only subtle sabotage of the Italian war effort. The women took up arms at one stage in Olymbos, beating off the Italian soldiers with sticks and tools used for breadmaking, but confrontation was rare.

Life got really hard when the Germans came. They had their victories in the Dodecanese, but knew they were facing defeat. The bombing of Germany and the scale of the defeats on the eastern front were common knowledge and now began the long retreat. They took what livestock they could and plundered everything that was moveable, caring little for the local people, who came close to starvation. In the winter of 1944 the British came too with fine quality flour and other staples and life could begin again. Those were the last days when the landscape was full of people, working like ants, I was told, to gain enough to eat. Many of the fishing boats did not even have nets, so fishing was done by spear, trident, petrol bomb and dynamite. Accidents were common. In the summer of 1946 villagers heard a huge explosion from the direction of Saria. They knew what had happened. They took their boats and found wreckage and bodies torn by prematurely exploded dynamite. On a rock, thrown there by the force of the explosion they found a two year-old baby girl, unscathed, unharmed, but very frightened. They took her back to the village and with her family gone she was taken in by relatives and well looked after. She lives in New York now, with one of her daughters and comes back to stay in the summer, an old, vivacious, lady, full of life. She speaks no word of English, always wears the old style clothes and loves the Big Apple.

In 1948 the British relinquished control of the Dodecanese and Karpathos was for the first time united with Greece. The civil war had its impact and the time of the Colonels was hard too, for the people of the north have always been independently minded, often radical and sometimes socialists. For decades they received little or no help from Athens. In 1971 the road from Diafani to Olymbos was opened, a dirt track at first, like that from Pigadia to the south. Then in 1980, electricity came and the village, a fairyland of oil lamps and candles at nightfall, lost some of its magic.

Throughout the last century the people here were not passive. While great forces swirled around them they went in search of adventure; to Iran, Morocco, Germany, France, Egypt, Russia and of course to the USA and the far north of Canada. At first they commuted back and forth, summer there, winter here, and then, as they grew more settled in America, they stayed longer. The first family to settle in Baltimore is reckoned to be that of Nikolaos Mastromanolis. He arrived there in 1947 and was joined by his wife and three children in 1954. Now, there are more than 300 families from Olymbos in Baltimore, most of them keeping the old traditions alive, through music and dialect, and using the internet, as well as locally produced newspapers.

It is impossible to say how long these traditions will continue. What cannot be denied is that there is some magnetic force keeping these independent, stubborn and difficult people together as they celebrate their cultural identity in a uniform world of flaccid, uniform people. Check their eyes their dark, oval eyes.

Kosmas

It is a painful and difficult thing to lose someone to mental illness; to see them change daily before your eyes, to glimpse, occasionally, the same old, sane person, to feel that somewhere inside that veil the old personality is still there. It is a painful thing. I have known this in another time, another world. With Kosmas it is different. Since I have known him, for more than twenty years, he has been sick, been on the outside, been unwell. But this is not a story of my loss, my pain, neither is it a story of sickness, of a descent into madness. No, it is a story of the triumph of an incredible personality as he has come to terms with his own illness, his limitations and the limitations of those around him and developed his personality to fill a unique and loved niche in the village. With Kosmas the village is a whole. Without him something is missing.

Kosmas was born 30th March 1953. I can be this precise because for many years he has sat before me, in this bar or that, with pencil and paper and with infinite care has written his name, Kosmas Georgios Manios, his date of birth and then three numbers. Now they are 48, 49, 50. If these figures puzzle you, they are his age. He is not quite sure of this so he brackets it neatly. 48, 49, 50. Then we see 185, his height in centimetres and 80 his weight in kilograms. I presume he knows the latter from his check-ups in the hospital in Rhodes. He goes there every year, *ya service*, we say, for a service and so that they can confirm he is unfit for work and sign papers so he can draw his pension.

He sits before me now, writing me a letter. When he is finished he will read it to me, slowly and carefully so that I can understand. Carefully and with dignity he will close the exercise book, put down the pencil and sit back, sipping his ouzo and then explain once again what he has written. Normally a request — shoes, a belt, something from England, often a football shirt — red, No 9, Manchester or Liverpool. Occasionally he surprises us all. I once left the island to go to a writing school. Kosmas wrote, *kalo vacation*, throwing in an unexpected French word to keep us on our toes, *kalo symposia* and he hoped I got 10 out of 10 and a "good" from the teacher. What can you say to that?

Kosmas is, supposedly, a schizophrenic. That's what the people of the village tell us anyway, but a German psychiatrist once told me this can be a catch-all term, describing a broad pattern of behaviour and opening the way to certain pharmaceuticals. He is the youngest of eight children, all whom have some kind of problem and he lives with his mother, a poor old lady, demented herself, in a small old stone house opposite the church. Years ago Kosmas would sit, in the morning, on the old wooden balcony, taking in the day. Gradually the balcony became more rickety and bits of it fell into the street below. Now it has become unusable so Kosmas sits in the open doorway, looking onto the street, one storey up. He doesn't seem to mind.

Kosmas' own word for his illness is *psychosy*. *Psychosy*, he says, *apo ton krio*. From the cold. He was in Canada, newly married; they had a small baby girl and he became ill from the cold. He laughs sometimes when he is drunk and I get him to talk about those days. There was snow everywhere, ice and snow, and it was cold and he became ill. We might laugh too, thinking of someone having a mental illness due to cold, but as we learn more about emigration and exile and the incidence of mental illness among immigrants, surely there are links, not necessarily to temperature, but to climate, to customs, to isolation and loneliness. In those days Kosmas worked in bars washing dishes, then in *hangdokia* and *fastfoodatigo*, serving gravy and mustard. If those two words fool you, please try again. *Hangdokia*, *fastfoodatigo*. They are gems of Greek American or Greenglish. *Handokia*, is a restaurant or bar that sells *handoki*, or in English hot dogs. OK? *Fastfoodatigo* you have now figured out is fast food to go. They decline these nouns in good grammatical Greek. The émigrés have many jokes like this. The Greek word for pimp is *ruffiano*, so the Greeks that worked fixing roofs, heard the Americans talking about roofers and called themselves *ruffianos*. If your speciality in America was floors you worked on *to floori*. There is much word play at the interface between the cultures.

So, Kosmas, in a strange, cold, country, far from this village, went mad, no doubt scaring near to death his young wife. She left with the baby and he was alone. A nightmare in the cold of Canada. His stories of those days concern fights and prostitutes who stole his money. One Eskimo girl even stole his trousers. A kindly police officer found him a spare pair and gave him the bus fare back to his room. He drank, washed dishes and went mad 5000 miles from home. How he got back here I do not know; my guess is that the Canadians deported him. I just remember him being around the village in tattered clothes, always ridiculed, always in the background and then, by some strange chemistry, we became friends. I was not being altruistic, I just wanted to improve my Greek and wanted to talk to someone in the evening when I was having a drink. Kosmas had no short-term memory at the time and was perfectly happy to answer the same question time and time again. How old are you? Where were you born? Do you have any children? What is your name? All the standard text book stuff. Kosmas would answer me time and time again with patience and clarity. Unfortunately also with a thick local accent, which I still have today. It amuses the people of the village that I talk with their tongue.

So, every night we fell into meeting Kosmas, and I. We would share a bottle or two of retsina, eat a little food and discuss the meaning of life and how much pension he got. As we became friends his personality began to emerge from under his defensive cloak. Other villagers would join us and Kosmas, slowly, slowly began to thrive. He developed two or three tricks, unique to himself, with which he is very pleased and with them he amuses the party. Maybe when all this started he was a figure of fun, but now he has got us all doing it and he just smiles to see us happy. The easiest to describe is the football match. Kosmas gives an imagined, invented commentary on a football game, but a game from long ago, a game sprinkled with names like Beckenbauer, Cruyff, Neeskens, Milla, Lev Yassim, names from before his illness, names he would have heard on the radio in his youth. These games are full of incident and the commentary goes at high speed, with great excitement and much hilarity from the crowd gathered around. Kosmas will occasionally throw in unexpected phrases . . . *To megalo speaker einai Kosmas* (the chief reporter is Kosmas), or the match is sponsored by Gillette, and we laugh and the joke gets spread through the village. After twenty minutes, or so, we are exhausted, we beg him to stop. He slows down, announces the final score. No matter how many goals are scored this always turns out to be one-one. He stops and sits back with that quiet grin. Nodding his grizzled head he looks round at the crowd, drinks his drink, smiles, drinks. He is satisfied. He belongs.

Another party piece is less easy to explain. Kosmas reads aloud. Menus, notices, advertisements. Kosmas reads them aloud. This might not sound much fun, but he has a special technique. Kosmas reads the English script as if it were Greek. For example the English P in the Greek script is *rho*, pronounced R. Our C is the hard Greek K. So cappuccino is pronounced in Kosmas' private tongue as *karrukino*. Yoghurt by an equally tortured logic is *youyouvity*. We first noticed this when there was a news report, on the television in the bar, concerning a corrupt Cretan banker called Koskotais. Kosmas heard this, turned to me and asked why this man's name was written on the menu. I was confused, but he pointed to cocktails, which by an incredible coincidence is pronounced Koskotais in this invented language. Kosmas was not phased by this at all, just assumed he was in the forefront of some new media. When he learnt that what he did amused us, he just included his reading skills in his repertory for a quiet Saturday night. By doing this Kosmas has turned a disadvantage into an advantage. He plays a central role in the company as, in his quiet, dignified way, with an air of total innocence, he reads a menu to a group of friends who crack up and roll around with laughter. What's interesting to me is that we all copy him. On several occasions I have found myself confronted by a confused waitress in a sophisticated Italian coffee bar in London as she tries to interpret my request for a mid-morning *karrukino*.

Much of the music and traditions in the village concerns *mandinades*. These are songs, sometimes spontaneous, often improvised, that are developed and sung on special occasions. The father of Kosmas, Georgios Manios, was the author of many famous *mandinades*. Before he died he taught them to Kosmas. Many of them have romantic names, *Trulakas, Signiori Brigandieri, Steno*. Kosmas likes to sit and write them out for me in his laborious schoolboy handwriting. He then reads them. If he is drunk he sings them. Kosmas has a voice of the authentic blues, deep, broken, strained, a voice of loneliness and suffering, exile and regret. When he sings you feel his pain. The *mandinades* he writes down for me are collectors' items, liquid poetry, verbal games, people's history. They tell of flocks of sheep and fields across the straits between the islands and the swords and the knives that tear your heart as you gaze at the mountains and long to be with your sheep, be on your lands. Maybe these words were written in our village, maybe in Manhattan or Canada. The feeling is the same; loneliness, exile and loss. The *mandinada, Signiori Brigandieri,* is the most famous ever written. It is social history. It tells the true story of an event during the Italian occupation, of a festival called by the Italians to celebrate some master stroke of their empire. All the local musicians were summoned. They did not know what to do; they had to go, they had to perform, to celebrate, to be seen to enjoy themselves. They arrived sad and confused. They sat in a circle, drank a little, joked in a restrained way. The Italian commandant sat there smiling. Then Kosmas' father picked up his lyre and sang.

> Welcome *Signore* the *Brigandieri*
> You are a wonderful Brigand
> We give you a thousand welcomes
> We hope that you love our beautiful island and
> We hope that you will never see your homeland again

They laughed, they strained to listen. The fat *Commandante* smiled benignly. He was popular, *il Duce* was great, and the people rolled about as the *mandinada* made fun of him in double entendres and the *Commondante* beamed and misunderstood everything. So there was a festival; the people could rejoice. They had found a way of beating their rulers, not with force of arms, but with comedy. Their weapon of choice.

Kosmas explains this to me for the tenth, maybe the twentieth, time and I nod and I smile as our roles are reversed and I become the village simpleton as he becomes the professor. He sits there animated, nodding, smiling, unshaven, unbeaten. A sick man; a proud man; a man in his own right; a man with humour. He was being teased once by a friend of mine. After putting up with this for too long, he turned and said 'Hey, don't you know you have a problem? Why don't you take some of my medicine'.

Kosmas depends on the generosity of others. He wears raggedy clothes; at least three shirts, bell bottom jeans from 1970, shoes, no socks. He seems content. He is a unique and special person who has overcome handicap and disadvantage and become someone in the village. Kosmas will never take sides. When we watch a game on the TV he will support both teams, AEK, or Panathanaikos, or Olympiakos, it doesn't matter. He will even wear two or three teams shirts, one on the other. A yellow one with a black eagle, a white one with a cockerel and sometimes, at the bottom, a red one with Liverpool FC.

He has learnt to hide his vulnerability, his soft, damaged self. Occasionally, however, with alcohol or stress, the shield is pulled aside. I asked him one time to come to London with me. It was a joke, but I wanted to practise my Greek for passport, for travel and so on. I pressed him. I pressed. I pressed.

Come with me, I said

I cannot.

Why not? I said Why not?

Kosmas became agitated. I learnt the Greek I wanted, but I also learnt.

It's all right for you. You have skills, you speak languages, I have nothing, I know nothing. I can go nowhere.

I looked deep into his troubled face, sat silently, sad for Kosmas, sad for myself. I paid the bill. I went home to bed.

Another time, sitting quietly with Kosmas the evening before I was due to depart for the winter, he seemed far away. I asked him what he was thinking about.

Nothing, he said. Nothing

So I pushed him again. Kosmas, what are you really thinking about?

Loneliness, he said, I am thinking of loneliness

Those words are with me still. They will not go away.

So he is a complex man, our Kosmas, and suffers a great deal. Often as he paces about the village he has a haunted look and you can see he is very ill. Alcohol makes him feel better and tobacco too. I have read that schizophrenics often cannot differentiate between the various signals that come to them. Music in the background, voices in the foreground and conversations addressed to them are of the same intensity, muddied and confused. Nicotine helps to separate these competing signals and enables Kosmas to make some sense of what is going on around him. Understandably, Kosmas smokes a great deal and he suffers for this; his lungs are a mess, his chest has collapsed and, as with all smokers, his back is curved.

The last time I saw Kosmas was in Rhodes in the Karpathos *cafeneion* on the main square. It was in the evening and they had given him an ouzo cocktail with fruit and a little umbrella. We talked for a while and Kosmas told me Rhodes was a good place for a holiday. The sea was warm, the people were kind.

We arranged to meet the next day, but he didn't show up.

The Boots

It is rewarding to live in a small community and watch it slowly reveal itself, to notice how this person begins to seem important or that one shallow. You notice physical things too; the changes in the weather, the arrival of passerines, the first tourists, but it's the people that fascinate. It is interesting to get to know them and notice how your opinions change over the years, but it is difficult too. For if you don't feel as close to someone as you did, or if you get closer to another, which of you has changed? Were you too swift to make judgement? Was your behaviour off-putting or were you just wrong?

One of my early pleasures in the village was to go to Anna's of an evening, to sit in the dark and listen to the old men talking. Now, I am one of those old men and contribute to the conversations. Of late I have taken to sitting with Manolis, a kindly old man with a lovely soft voice and gentle manners. Sometimes he will have an ouzo with me, or a coffee, or one of Anna's special teas, made from herbs that she gathers in the mountains. Usually he is sitting there first and, following the local tradition, if he invites me to sit at his table, then he has to pay. By eight o'clock he is ready to leave, but by then we have had half an hour of pleasant conversation and I have practised my Greek and maybe improved a little. We have spoken before, of course. Sometimes on the beach, where Manolis, in common with other villagers of his age, takes the advice of the local doctors and goes for an afternoon dip. But the truth is that I knew very little about him until recently. He was a beekeeper once and still keeps a few hives and calmly and politely explains to me how and when to do this and that. One of the problems with keeping bees here is that everyone, beekeeper or not, thinks they are an expert and they give advice with great authority and passion. If they do this in the *cafeneion* then they are overheard and another expert steps in to explain

No, no, no, that will kill them all. What you have to do is . . .

And an argument starts and you learn nothing, except perhaps a few new curses that you did not know before, or perhaps some new names for intimate parts of the human anatomy.

Manolis is not like that. He will ask questions and recall that he had the same problem once with his bees. Not to worry, if you follow this procedure then everything will be fine. And speaking softly, in slow dialect, or in broken English, he will explain exactly what to do. So I enjoy our conversations and gradually, in a shy way, we have become friends.

One evening, without warning, he surprised me and I learnt another of the village stories.

You are not the first Englishman here you know. There was another long ago. Kevy. Kevy Andrew.

Who?

Kevy Andrew.

Kevin Andrews?

Yes. Kevin Andrews.

He was here? Kevin Andrews came here?

Of course.

Now Kevin Andrews wrote *the* great book about Greece in the immediate aftermath of the Second World War, when it was riven by a deep and vicious civil conflict. *The Flight of Ikaros* deals not only with this difficult and ugly period in European history, but also with the friendship between Greek peasant people and the young Kevin Andrews, an urbane, sophisticated American.

And he was here?

Yes. He sat where you are sitting now. He sat in that very chair. He was a friend of mine. Like you he loved this place and like you he loved to walk in the country. He asked me to make him some boots and I made him some.

You make boots?

Of course. I used to be a boot maker, but now I am retired....

Manolis continues and explains that Kevin Andrews first came here in the sixties and walked everywhere over the north of the island. He loved the place because it was wild and remote and was loved by everyone in return. In *The Flight of Ikaros* he writes of playing the shepherd's flute and yes, Manolis confirms, he was better than the locals and his Greek was perfect. He even wrote *mantinades* and they are remembered today. Manolis wrote two of them down for me. One was about the village and the other was about the wind. Later that night the wind tore them from my hand and took them away. Somehow this felt appropriate.

The process of writing a *mantinada* is rarely a solo effort and several people, who was there at the time, explained to me.

We were there in the *cafeneion*, trying to help him choose the right words and suddenly they came and we had a new *mantinada*.

> Now, I have decided I am Olymbitic
> Because I, myself am iron
> And your place, magnetic.

Around the village many people remember Kevin. There are many stories about him, including one that he was a spy. There is no surprise in this. In those days all strangers were viewed with suspicion and it was never explained who they thought he was spying for. One of his daughters, Ioanna, came too in the seventies and she is also remembered fondly. There is a darker side. Kevin Andrews suffered greatly from epilepsy, an illness not fully understood in this village at that time and once or twice he needed help from rather frightened and concerned villagers as they came across him on one of the many footpaths and donkey tracks. And the boots, or *stibania* as they are called in the old language here, well Kevy thought they were wonderful.

So, I did a little research on Kevin Andrews and found that he fought in Italy in the Second World War with the American Army and afterwards he settled in Greece. Here he wrote and married and had children. During the time of the Colonels he wrote articles protesting the lack of freedom under this quasi-fascist dictatorship. He was arrested, beaten up and his arm was broken in the siege at the Polytechnic in Athens. He maintained his solidarity with the people of Greece. When the Colonels were replaced with a semblance of a democratic regime, Kevin Andrews took out Greek citizenship and, when he found out that the Americans still considered him a citizen, he publicly renounced that status in order to protest against the support that the Americans had given the Junta. Kevin Andrews, a strong swimmer, drowned while swimming off Kythira in 1989.

And Manolis? Well his story is interesting too. There have only been a handful of boot makers on this island, as this style of boots were not introduced until the end of the nineteenth century. He learnt this trade and made a living until the seventies, when times were hard. Then he went to America where he worked in a restaurant in Baltimore; managing, cooking, anything. A hard life for a not young man with not very good English. He was telling me his story when Anna came over with a large parcel.

The postman has been and brought you some leather.

I don't like clichés, but like a dog, my ears pricked up.

Why do you need leather?

A pause. A hint of a smile. A low, modulated voice.

Well I still make boots, you know. Occasionally

Frantic and confused thoughts, the cost, the foolishness, the etiquette. I don't want them cheap because we are friends. The language. How do I explain?

Boreis na mou kaneis merika? Can you make me some?

A broad smile.

Just like I made for Kevy?

Just the same.

And I have them now. My feet and calves were measured and a week later I tried them on and they were a perfect fit. Too rich red and too yellow suede for discreet everyday wear, but perfectly made, soft as a babies skin with tops that roll up and down and can be worn under trousers or over. The souls are made of tyres from a truck and my *stibania* are waterproof and warm even in the rain and the snow. A vanity perhaps, certainly a conceit, but what the hell. Just like Kevin Andrews and a lasting memory of a good friend.

The Gays

Visitors often ask me about the Greek attitude to sex. This is a strange question when you think about it, sex being one of those things which link together all of mankind — and a good thing too. I am not an expert on comparative social attitudes, but I think there is a tolerance in our villages that is unexpected and welcome. We have many foreigners living among us; Albanians, Bulgarians, Egyptians, even the occasional English eccentric. All are welcome. They are exploited, of course, as all refugees and outcasts are exploited everywhere, but then we exploit one another. Thus, it can be said, that foreigners are treated as equals.

In the summer many different kinds of visitors arrive, some with outrageous or unknown sexuality. They have pins through their noses, their eyebrows, their ears and maybe other places too; they wear strange clothes, especially the women, and they sit in our bars and even in our *cafeneion*, with shaven heads and big boots and they roll their own cigarettes like cowboys in old films. Such people arouse curiosity, amusement and speculation, but so long as they respect our attitudes to nudity and to public displays of affection they are tolerated and welcomed. Where they can, our people will find ways to fit strangers into our society. The Greek word for foreigner, *Xenos*, is the same as the Greek word for guest. We are proud of this and the responsibility it places on us to make visitors feel welcome.

A story that I like concerns two gay men who came to a village further south from here. The older, a very handsome and quite famous actor was Greek and his partner was a young Englishman. They wanted to follow the dream of many urban people; to live in a village, to lead what is mistakenly called the simple life. They searched the island from north to south. Our village was too strange for them, too cut-off, the life here was too hard. They went to other villages and other islands. They stayed, they looked, they moved on. Eventually they found a place they liked, hidden in the fold of a mountain like our women hide sweets for young children in their skirts. I will not name it, but this place is a gem. In the spring there is water and there are flowers, there is birdsong, there are trees and there is peace. Only local people own land and houses there. They keep flocks of sheep and goats, they make cheese and yoghurt and those things, like curds and whey, that you used to hear about in fairy stories, but no longer understand. Only a few people live there all the year round; there are empty houses, some in ruins, and one of these appealed to our gay friends.

This is a small, isolated community and the gay couple neither wanted to offend sensibilities, nor to be rejected because of their sexuality. They paid many visits to the hamlet, talked to the old people with respect, talked to the owner of the property and after much bargaining and hesitation on both sides, agreed a price. The dance they led was like the gavotte they have in films about the old times in Europe — now this way, now that, a bow, a circle, a coffee here, a visit there. Finally, the property was theirs. They drew up plans, sought permissions, arranged for money from the bank, but they were not sure. They loved this little house, but the gamble was big. They were vulnerable.

The time came to arrange for builders. They took a risk, they invited Phillipos to come to the house, to sit in the courtyard, to drink an ouzo, take a *meze* and discuss a contract. Phillipos was not the oldest man in the village, but he was held in much respect. Phillipos had been to America, been a builder. He is a big man, tall and strong with a magnificent moustache, and his deep, brown eyes penetrated theirs and his laughter filled the afternoon. They sat, they drank, they talked, they drank some more. Phillipos liked the plans. He could do the work. He would do the work. The sun had gone now, dark shadows reached the house while the stones in the little courtyard clicked and ticked with the heat from the day. They sat in the dark, unspoken thoughts in their minds, watching the small pool of light from the one oil lamp. There was silence, then cicadas. Sheep moved in the mountain, a mouse ran by and then silence again.

Phillipos played with his moustache; the corners of his eyes creased and his eyes glinted.

Do you have any brothers? He asked the English.

No.

Do you? He asked the Greek.

Unfortunately not.

Silence again, then . . . Ah! Said Phillipos, gently. Then you are two brothers who have found one another.

A pause, then a smile, then laughter. Then lots of laughter. They poured another ouzo. They looked at one another. It was going to be all right. They were home.

The Musician

How long have I known Manolis Balaskas? Could it be twenty years ago that we first met? He was a taxi driver then, in New York, but still made the annual pilgrimage each Easter to the village to meet friends and family and to play music. He seemed much older than me in those days, but now I feel that we are the same age. He still drives a taxi, but in Rhodes , which means he comes home to the village much more frequently. He looks the same; that big nose, those bushy eyebrows are still there and the big frame, though a shade bent. His hands have not changed; strong hands, musician's hands, fast skilful and gentle, capable of rhythm and grace.

I describe Manolis as a taxi driver, but he is not. He is a musician, one of the most important musicians in the community. He plays the *lauto* (lute) and the *lyra,* a three stringed instrument, bowed like a violin, but held vertically and with small bells on the bow to give a hint of syncopation. Like all the major musicians here, he makes his instruments, both *lyra* and *lauto,* with his own hands. This is like expecting a member of the Berlin Philharmonic to make their own violin, but more difficult. A *lauto* is more complex than a violin and in his life he has made four. There may be other musicians who are, in some way, better than Manolis, faster, more rhythmic, cleverer with *manti-*

nada, but, I would argue, nobody has done more to maintain the traditional style of playing which matters so much to this small community. Manolis is not flash; he is elegant and cultured.

The best music here is not performance; it is ceremony. Nobody applauds, they participate. This is communal art. It exists as an organic and living entity without external support, or subsidy. Without people like Manolis it would die. The tradition is to let the music unfold appropriately to the occasion. At a major *panagiry* (church festival), for example, the men will gather, sit together and drink. After a while a *lyra* and a *lauto* will appear and *mantinades* are sung. Typically the oldest man there will sing a *mantinada* of welcome, maybe singling out a special guest with recently composed verses. Someone, maybe that special guest, will respond with their improvised verses and we are off, rhythmic, compelling, call and response improvisation, trills and flights on the lyra, rhythm from the lute and, slightly off the beat, the sound of the men's feet slapping on the floor. Sometimes the men will sing of the sad things that have happened to them and they will cry. This is a catharsis or cleansing of the emotions. Sometimes the *mantinades* are beautifully written. You would find it hard to improve on the following rage against the passing of years by Andreas Hirakis, a shepherd from Olymbos.

I want to let out a shrill cry against the wind's backbone.
I grieve, I weep, I cry out loud that old age has come.

At other times they will sing of the island and its topography. The sea is always wild at one place to the north and they might sing

Troulakas, ugly and black with your terrible places.
Many a problem you caused in the old peoples faces.

And together they will remember the times when they rowed and sailed their heavy wooden boats laden with people and goats from Diafani to Saria or to Tristomos and they will remember their fathers and their grandfathers too.

As the women gather, the songs will change, as will the tempo of the music. This will change to dance tunes and the older men will, in a gesture lost to the West, dance with their daughters and dance with their granddaughters, collectively in a circle, demonstrating and leading the way and showing off too. For who could resist showing to your favourite granddaughter that you can still dance and can she imagine how good you were when you were young and her mother not yet born?

As hours go by the music does not stop, not for one second. Music is eternal, forever, and so is the drinking. On we go and everyone in the village is there. Everyone who can will dance round and round, holding hands in a long line. One two, three, skip, four. One two, three, skip four. The music does not stop. Manolis and Minas and Georgos and other men from the village sit round tables in the middle of the dancers. The musicians will be up on chairs on the tables. Perhaps with two *lauto* now, perhaps a *tsambouna* (bagpipe) too. But the music will not stop. As each musician tires, the tune continues as they are replaced by another man. These days Manolis can play for only three or maybe four hours before he needs to rest and to wash his hands in neat whisky, to burn out the pain and bring back feeling. Others replace him, but the music goes on and the dancers go round and the feet go slap, slap, slap.

Depending how is the *glendi* (range of emotions expressed) and how good is the *kefi* (feeling of well being) that people are having, this can go on for eighteen or twenty hours, or even on some special occasion, for days. Everyone participates. They sing verses of *mantinada*, or the chorus, they play an instrument, or they dance. There is no applause; this it is not a performance, it is a collective experience, an affirmation of village life.

Manolis and others teach the young people, as they were taught by their fathers, the tunes, the verses, the oral traditions. Others teach how to dance, or how to wear the traditional dress and what it signifies. Wherever the diaspora has taken these people — New York, Rhodes, Baltimore, Piraeus or Canada — they maintain their traditions fiercely in the face of powerful and competing interests. This music is centuries old. It is living, evolving, exquisite and unique. It is culture, not mass culture; it is not entertainment. And this man sitting up high, on a rough stool on a simple wooden table, well into the night, this gentle man, was a taxi driver in New York. Think of the film by Scorsese and you will understand why, when we first met, I asked, how he could live such a double life. I would not ask now. I understand that he had to work to eat and to feed his family and that he lived to play music and to strengthen and preserve the traditions of the village and that the village too was his family.

We think of these things as we sit quietly by the sea in the late afternoon. Manolis plays *lyra* and sings gentle songs of love and of longing, of loneliness, exile, birth and death. He is older than me once again. He is tired. He stops playing. He yawns. There is silence and I hear the wind in the tamarisk tree. We sit there and think of a time when his music will stop and will not start again and we wonder who will tell his story and who will sing his song and we wonder if anyone will listen. We sit there and think of these things, but we say nothing.

The Golden Beach

To watch a football match on television, in a bar in our village, is to be amused, intimidated, frightened and confused. If you are a foreigner it gets worse. What on earth is going on? Arms are raised, tempers are lost, men stand up and shout, point at the television angrily, sit down and laugh; drinks are ordered, children come and go.

Penalty

It's not a penalty

Offside

Not offside

Foul.

It's not a foul.

All this at the top of their voices. And of course all of one team has the same name, *malakas* (wanker). So, it's this *malakas* did this and that *malakas* did that. The other team also have the same name, but only when a goal is missed or a pass goes astray does the cry *malakas* go up and arms are waved and hands pointed. The referee, of course, is aloof from all this. He is known as *o megalos malakas* (the big wanker) and treated with the respect allowed to all referees throughout the world. You will be surprised to find that every one of our customers has perfect eyesight. They can see half way round the world, on a small screen, better than the referee (*o megalos malakas*) can see ten metres from the play.

Foul

Not a foul

It's a foul

It's not a foul

Eisai malakas

Ego? Ochi, eisai megalos malakas.

I think you understand the point. They see perfectly, they just see different things perfectly. Supposedly, science was invented in Greece. How? There is no tradition of dispassionate, objective observation in Greece that I can detect. How did these people produce Pythagorus and Euclid, let alone Socrates? Talking of Socrates leads us to the incredible conspiracy that exists at all levels, in all countries, in all sports. Race plays a part in these conspiracies, as does money and politics. The conspiracy exists to deprive small nations, mainly those with Greek or Serb populations, with great skills and not enough money, of their just rights. No mistakes are made, there are no differences of opinion, no decisions are arrived at independently. Instead it's:

Berlusconi was on the phone

Blair told FIFA to do this

The Mafia

The Russian Mafia

And my favourite? In a world cup match between England and Brazil, a Brazilian player was sent off. Clearly, I was told, because of an Israeli, British, American conspiracy. I mean, they actually believed that George W had taken time off from conquering the world to help out Tony Blair by fixing the match. And Israel? Well, maybe the Mexican referee had a Jewish grandmother. How do I know?

But pause for a second. Something real is happening here. If you watch carefully you may learn something of the Greek character. There is incredible social interaction.

These people may support different teams, or hold opposing political views; they may not even like one another, or their families, but together they are enjoying a match. They are not sitting alone at home with their cans of beer, quietly cursing, analysing and praying. They are here in the bar, laughing, shouting and screaming, waving their arms and swearing and taking part in a drama, a collective drama. Now the Greeks did invent drama. There's Aeschylus, Sophocles, Euripides, not to mention Aristophanes. And now we have Dimitris and Nikos and Vasillis and Georgos. So, why not join in? Sit down. Relax. Lets have a beer, or an ouzo.

Did you see that?
Offside.
Not offside
Was offside
Eisai malakas
Ego? Malakas? Ego?
There. Don't you feel good?

Steno

So now we are going on a little trip, not far, just an hour or so, but also off the end of the world and there I will fish.

As we leave the village it is four o'clock. We head north. The weather is not too bad, about six or seven Beaufort, but the wind is strong enough, the boat is small and we have to be careful. The weather is coming from the northwest, they call it Maestros, and I check the fuel tank as we tuck in under the cliffs, out of the wind. *Yialo, yialo* they say. Close to the coast.

As we go north we pass places where huge rocks, coffee coloured and grey, tumble into the sea, scattered among them pine trees, tall and green. We pass by places I know. I love the names; Vananda, Calamnia, Kamara, Kabo. At the cape (Kabo) there are Eleanora's falcons; above them and above the cliffs, black against the sky, there are eagles. These falcons are incredible birds, the ultimate tourists. They winter, mainly, in Madagascar; in January they head out across Africa, then north across the Sahara to Morocco and the straits of Gibraltar. There they feed on passerines, the small birds of passage struggling north to Europe. The Eleanoras rest, then head east to Sicily and Sardinia, feeding on small birds and insects on the way. It was here that they picked up their name. In the sixteenth century, Princess Eleanora of Sardinia loved them so much that she had them incorporated into her shield; their proud, royal features still look out from the family crest. Late April sees them arriving on our island, in ones and twos, beating against the wind, a metre or two above the waves, taking advantage of the uplift provided by the ocean. They are above us now, swooping, diving, playing games of chase, showing off, having fun. We hear their cries, but at a distance. Tonight they will be closer and I will continue their story.

The sea is a little rough, the current going north meets the wind coming round the coast and it is choppy. The sea is very deep here, so the waves are deep blue with fringes of white, soapy foam. The cliffs tower above, purple and brown, and small pine trees cling there like bonsai in a Japanese rock garden. The waves are enough to worry about, but I take care. *Yialo, yialo,* inside this rock, outside that. I shelter, look, move out into the wind as it curves round the cliffs. *Yialo, yialo.*

We pass Mavri Petra (black rock) and Troulakas, which has it's own poem and move on to Alona. There it will be windy and it is, very, very windy, but these days I know what I am doing. I have been here before. There are cormorants here including one special variety, with a special scientific name. *Phalacorakas Aristotelis* should give you a clue as to who first identified this species. Princesses and philosophers name our birds. I pass inside the little island of Amoi. Here, two hundred years ago, lepers were isolated and their cells can still be seen. Among the ghosts live Audouin's gulls. More recently, when Reagan and Gorbachov were seeking ways of doing sensible things about nuclear weapons, two young boys from the village wrote to these, supposed world leaders. They said they were from the island of Amoi and wanted to be invited, as a third world power representing youth, to discuss peace. Neither Reagan, nor Gorbachov replied.

We are at Steno now and it is wild. It is always wild here. The wind from the west drives the sea into the narrow and shallow straits between the islands of Karpathos and Saria. There is not enough room for all that water and the sea piles up into waves that pound and shake my little boat. For years I could go no further than this. To me it was, literally, the end of the world and I would look north to Saria or west to the open sea, lose my courage and turn back again. Then I learnt how to cross the straits safely; head west at first, keep close in and shelter behind those rocks, edge out into the channel and turn, slowly, slowly, so that the wind is from behind, *prima, prima*. Easy now, not too fast, then edge close to Saria and we are on the other side and safe for a while longer.

Saria is owned by the people of our village. It is a wild, dry, historic, landscape; there are olive trees here and beehives, sheep that roam free and wild goats that feed from the mountain herbs. It is uninhabited for most of the time, but our people used to live here, for the summer at least. In the spring they would drive the animals, cows, sheep, donkeys, goats, horses, mules, to the north of Karpathos, to the narrowest crossing between the islands. There they would load the small ones onto boats and tie the larger ones behind to swim, then they would row across this wild channel, with much shouting and encouragement and beating of water. The older animals had learnt to swim against the current, the younger were confused and panicked and some were lost. Off they would go, animals men and women in boats, animals in the sea, rowing and swimming against wind and waves, 70, 80, 100 metres to Saria, safety, relief, dry land and fresh pasture. In the autumn they would reverse the operation and return south. The old people still talk of those times; the animals, the confusion, the curses, the songs they sang. Some film company came thirty years ago and asked them to re-enact the scene. Off they went and relived their youth. It was a great film. It is in some archive somewhere, but you will never see it. City people protested about cruelty to animals and the project was shelved. Nobody protested about cruelty to our villagers, who worked hard and risked their lives for historic record and, of course, were not paid.

Think about these things as we head north on the east coast of Saria. Perhaps you can hear the music of memories above the wind, or maybe it's just in my mind, as we pass Mairias and Asproas. The sea is calm now and here we will fish, for I am hungry for soup. I know the place, I have been here before and we fish with *katheti*, the vertical line with four hooks.

We catch plenty of *hannos*, a few *perka* and even a fine *scorpios,* the big, red, ugly fish with poisoned spikes along its back fins and gills. I have time to think too, to contemplate the island of Saria, the people who lived there, the unknown people who live there still. I have been surprised to find young boys guarding sheep, or old women sitting in the shade of rude, stone houses, in olive groves. The greeting is always the same — sit for a while, have some water, what news from the village, do you want to stay? It has been thus for centuries, perhaps for more than forty centuries. That is our heritage. There are no roads in Saria, no cars, no televisions. Without roads there is no use for the wheel; we use mules, donkeys and the bent backs of our people. At one time pirates lived here, perhaps from Syria, and before them there were monks and priests, and before them Minoans and Dorians, but always our people toiling away in the sun, making terraces, making soil, making fields, making those beautiful donkey tracks and footpaths that climb the highest mountains. For height gives you view and the further you could see, the longer the warning of pirates and other predators. The English came here in the 1850s in their big wooden ships. They reported nothing of interest. But they mapped the coastline, as they mapped the coastlines of the world, just in case the information was needed in some future war. And it was. Turks came, then Italians and Germans and, briefly, the English again, and then in 1948 the world decided what we had known all along. Saria and Karpathos belonged to Greece.

We have two and a half kilos of fish, enough for my family, and dusk approaches, so take in the line for the last time and we will head south. Steno again, calmer now, and as we turn west into the channel we turn into the sun, a huge blood orange falling between islands and rocks as a bank of white clouds masks the far horizon. Often, this time of day, the wind drops and for this I am grateful as in the dark it is difficult to see, difficult to steer. So there is tension as we return, keeping away from the dark cliffs, further out from unseen rocks. We pause a little at the cape, the Eleanoras are above us again, but mob handed now, fifty or more, diving, screaming, shouting, teasing us as they aim just above my head in the dark and fly out to sea, centimetres above the waves. These are smart birds. They lay eggs in August in scrapes and fissures in the cliffs above. Their young are born about now, the time that the passerines return from Europe. These little birds fly at night and eat in the day, but they like to hug the coast, so the Eleanoras sleep in the day and at night, at this place, they form a curtain, a net one or more kilometres out to sea, and there they wait. The little birds fly on in the dark until suddenly. . . whoosh, there are feathers on the sea and there is food for a young Eleanora.

The remaining passerines head south and so do we, using our senses in the dark, listening to the waves on rocks, the swish of the sea on the beach at Kalamnia. There is no moon, but the stars show themselves as the light fades from the sky and I use my face to feel the wind, to know which way to steer in the dark, and then there is the smell of the pine trees, borne by the wind down the valley at Vananda. Then I know we are nearly home and safe. I have to keep clear of the rock on the right, close to the cliff, then pass between the cliff and the rocks on the left. If there are waves I will hear them hit the rocks and the stars will show me the surf. Past the rocks and we are safe and home in the dark and ready for soup.

John

This story should not be in this book. It is not about our village, nor even our island. It is about an Englishman in Crete. However, we have much in common with Crete and for sure the English have helped us from time to time. In what you call the Second World War, for example, Greece and Britain stood alone against the Axis powers for nearly two years before the Americans joined in and even then it was Germany and Japan that declared war on the USA and not the other way round, as the Americans like to tell you. Those were dark times for the people of Karpathos. We were occupied by the Italians then, part of their Dodecanese empire, and while they did not treat us as badly as the Germans did later, some of our men were killed and others were tortured and bad things did happen. Collectively our forefathers decided that it would be foolish to resist openly on the island, but instead opted to go to the mainland and join with the communists and the nationalist resistance. Sixty men went from the village of Olymbos alone to fight the Germans in the wild mountains of the Pindos. There were volunteers from the other villages too, so we have nothing to be ashamed of in Karpathos, but it was wise not fight on our own island.

In Crete things were different. It is big enough and wild enough and rich enough for men to take to the hills and harry and resist invaders, be they Venetians, Turks or Germans. Cretans have been doing this for centuries and in May 1941 when German parachutists came out of the sky the Cretans went out and fought them. Armed with shotguns and blunderbusses, pistols, axes, knives and shovels, they went out into the olive groves and vineyards and fought alongside the British, the New Zealanders and the Australians. When they killed Germans they took their weapons and killed more Germans until they ran out of ammunition. The Germans had been told that the islanders would welcome them as liberators and were surprised by such resistance. The parachutists were butchered in such numbers, over 4000 were killed, that the Germans never again attempted a large-scale airborne landing. Unfortunately the efforts of the defenders were not good enough. Soldiers came by air and by sea, the Luftwaffe inflicted serious casualties, and very soon key airfields and ports were captured. Poor equipment, poor planning and poor leadership led to the defeat of the defending armies and the Germans soon took control of the northern coast and some of the larger villages inland. The British and their allies either surrendered or retreated overland and with the assistance of Cretan irregulars escaped through the Gorge of Samaria and other places on the south coast. There they were taken off by boat and submarine and escaped to Egypt.

Not all of the allies left. Some who could not escape, or refused to surrender, took to the hills and the mountains and joined with local shepherds and bandits, patriots and freedom fighters. Together they resisted the occupiers and did what the Cretans have in their blood to do; kill and run, resist, escape, harry and hide. The country people of Crete can live for days on hard, salty, sheep's cheese, a handful of small, black olives and dried bread. Most of them have rifles and guns and they know how to hunt for food or kill for vendetta. Their clothes in those days were made for the mountains; the boots and baggy trousers of the men protected them from the thorns and spiny bushes of the Cretan landscape and shepherds there have used caves for shelter for hundreds, if not thousands, of years. Cretans are born guerrilla fighters and a little crazy with it, they never give in; they do not know how to. The resistance began immediately, but it took some time before it was integrated into the strategy of the allies. In many parts of Greece the story was the same; a refusal to accept defeat, followed by passive resistance and then armed opposition to the invaders. This led, over a period of time, to full-scale insurrection throughout Greece and the expulsion of the Germans from parts of the mainland and to massive resistance in Crete and other islands. Many books have been written on the subject, but only those written by Greek authors have come close to telling the truth. British officers involved in the resistance tended to come from a narrow stratum of British society and, when they wrote their books and their memoirs and when they became professors after the war, they reflected the social and political views of that stratum and also of the British secret services. The resistance on the mainland was led mainly by the communists and their allies, in a broad front known as ELAS. Despite this, the British government backed the royalists at crucial moments in the war and sometimes behaved with great treachery towards the Greek people. The story on Crete was different. There were jealousies, infighting, mistakes and intrigue, but no major ideological splits occurred during the war, just a collective determination to rid the land of the invader.

Within months of the German victory in Crete, young British men were being dropped by parachute, or landed in rubber boats from submarines or *caiques* to assist and organise the resistance. The officers tended to be classics graduates from Oxford or Cambridge, whose public school background suited the spartan, male existence demanded by this irregular method of warfare. They spoke Greek too, but not modern Greek, nothing so practical. They spoke the Greek of Homer and Aristotle, Aeschylus and Aristophanes. Imagine being a shepherd in the hills and seeing young, foreign men come floating down from the sky and they speak to you in a form of your language obsolete for more than a thousand years. The British had radios and had contact with the Allied war effort and through them the Greek government in exile. They worked with bands of *andartes* and fought heroically in a bitter and bloody war. Few prisoners were taken by either side. The Germans did not understand or like this kind of fighting and took bloody and cruel reprisals against local men, women and children. They tried, but failed to intimidate the population. They never had full control of the island and in 1944 were preparing to pull out of Crete and start their retreat through Greece and Yugoslavia, a retreat in which, harassed all the way by determined resistance fighters who blew up bridges and train lines and viaducts, they were to suffer over 100,000 casualties. One of the last major actions of the war in Crete was the capture of General Kreipe and this is where my friend John comes in.

I was in Zakros, in the East of Crete, a quiet place off-season, with the remains of a wonderful Minoan palace. It was the layout of Zakros that appealed to the Minoans. It is by the sea that they loved so much and there is evidence of a simple harbour. Behind the beach is a fertile coastal plain and to this day intensive agriculture takes advantage of the rich, friable tilth and the small river that runs for much of the year down a narrow steep gorge. It is in this gorge that the Minoans left their dead, up high in caves, away from floods and animals. This place is still known as the Valley of the Dead.

John was staying at the same taverna as me. He was about sixty-five at the time, in the mid-eighties, and travelling with his partner, Gill, a younger woman who clearly cared for him a great deal. He was a shy man and it took me several days before he would tell me even a part of his story. We had a few drinks together one evening and towards the end of our conversation John asked me if I knew of any good walks in the area. I told him about the walk up the Valley of the Dead.

Cross over the stream, turn inland and up the valley. It is spectacular, quiet, wild and beautiful. But take care, it can be very hot.

Can we get a drink somewhere?

Take lots of water with you, but when you get to the top you are in the village of Ano Zakros. There is a small bar there where the taxi drivers drink. They will make you welcome.

I did not see them the next day and by the time they emerged the day after that I was sitting in the shade looking at the sea and having my mid afternoon beer.

How did it go?

Incredible.

Incredible?

Yes, incredible.

And they told me: It was hot, very, very hot, so when they emerged at the top of the valley they went straight to the bar. Cold beers on the table and, in the corner, an old man with a large, droopy moustache who, after the normal salutations, asked.

Are you German?

No. British.

The old man paid for the beers. British honour means that you buy one back and soon there was a *parea*, or little party, developing. In Crete, once they have established where you come from, how much money you earn and how many children you have, the conversation turns to war. Of course, after two or three beers, all Cretans are *andartes* and heroes, or that's what they tell you anyway.

So the old man started on a long and rambling story in hard to follow Cretan dialect, with a smattering of English army slang. All the time John had a strange sense of unease; not quite *déjà vu*, but certainly a feeling of familiarity. At the end they could not understand him until he took them outside and pointed to a mountain to the east and said, slowly, in his best Greek

In 1944, no matter the weather, I lived on that mountain and watched the German trucks and cars. I had a radio and every day I had to report what was going on to an English officer.

Then with dignity and genuine interest, tinged with a little local arrogance, he asked of John.

And what did you do in the war?

John paused for a while then, pointing to another mountain to the south said with great care in his best, long forgotten Greek.

I was on that mountain and I was the officer.

The old man couldn't believe it. Maybe there was a joke. He tugged at the corners of his moustache, stepped forward, looked directly into John's eyes and asked him to repeat what he had said.

I was on that mountain. I was the English officer. You were reporting to me.

The old man stood still for a few seconds while he tugged at his moustache again. Then, he seized John by the shoulders and kissed him on both cheeks and then fully on the lips. He kissed Gill too, but only on the cheeks and then, stepping back two paces, stood to attention and slowly gave a smart British army salute. Suddenly all three of them were laughing and crying, singing and hugging one another and then, following the lead of the old man, they began to dance; a slow Cretan dance from distant memory. After a while the customers in the bar began to notice and shouted to them to ask what was going on. So they went back into the dark, smoky bar and the story was told and retold and beers came and bottles were emptied and then it was time for *tsikoudia*, the Cretan *eau de vie,* and when Cretans start on the spirits you had better watch out. Songs of love and war were sung and *mantinades* composed to suit the occasion and to spin the story. Old men came out of their houses with four string Cretan *lyres* and with lutes that they had made themselves many years before.

By now half the village had gathered and soon young men were dancing on tables and plates and bottles were thrown at walls for celebration. Tall, dark, Cretan beauties gathered to look in the windows of the bar. Later they would be chased by boys and would run away until far from the bar, in the moonlight, they allowed themselves to be caught. Guns in Crete are never far away and as the night drew on and the frenzy mounted, the stars became targets. None were hit, but the noise was tremendous and the whole village was awake. It continued like this until dawn. Then, one of the taxi drivers who had gone outside to escape this mayhem and commotion and fallen asleep in a neighbour's goat shed woke up. He came into the bar brushing dirt and dung and vine leaves from his frayed jumper and baggy trousers. He surveyed the broken plates and smashed bottles, the beer running across the floor and dripping into the street, the comatose bodies and John and Gill sitting quietly in the corner holding hands while a happy, ancient warrior snored away at their table. He signalled to them to follow, got them into his taxi and slowly and carefully drove them down the hill and back to Zakros. They arrived as the deep red sun rose through thin white clouds floating over Homer's wine dark sea.

So John, with assistance from Gill, began to tell me his story. This was his first visit to Greece since 1945. And yes, he had been one of those brave young men who dropped so surprisingly from the sky. His job was to work with the resistance in the east of the island. Unlike the other Brits in those days he spoke modern Greek well, having been brought up in the twenties at the famous Villa Ariadne just outside Heraklion, the very same house that General Kreipe was occupying in 1944. The east of Crete is less mountainous and not as rugged as the rest of the island and the resistance there was passive. To protect the local people from reprisals there were no ambushes and no attacks on German outposts. The brief was to liaise, watch and report. I asked him about the kidnap of Kreipe. What John said was quite shocking to me and I would not repeat the story if I thought he was still with us. I have read all the published reports of this operation and they tell of a daredevil attack and kidnap and how Kreipe was stopped at a roadblock by British officers dressed as Germans, captured, carried south through the Samara Gorge and taken by submarine to Egypt. Demoralised and leaderless the Germans hastened their retreat and the whole operation was, supposedly, a great success.

John's story was different.

It was a gong hunting expedition, he told me. It should never have happened.

In the latest books there is some reappraisal of the events, but nothing as blunt as this. John told me that the Germans knew they were beaten and that informal negotiations had been going on with the British and Greeks for a peaceful withdrawal of the Axis forces. The local people did not want a bitter and vengeful occupying force to implement a burnt earth policy as they left. Winters are hard in Crete and the *andartes* were willing to let the Germans leave peacefully in order to save their crops and their houses. John's view was that the operation was foolhardy; it delayed the withdrawal and needlessly caused the loss of lives of good people. He told me of German reprisals on the Lasithi Plateau, further west from Zakros, of the murder of 400 villagers of all ages and the burning down of villages and farmhouses. He was a bitter man. It was his job to put the resistance organisation in the east of Crete back together again. The *andartes* were furious. Their homes and crops were destroyed, their families and friends murdered, for no reason at all. Despite this John managed to get his end of the island organised again, an important achievement, not only to see the Germans out in an orderly fashion, but to maintain order when peace came. In the chaos of war vendettas and revenge attacks are to be expected on families and fighters who had, truly or supposedly, betrayed one another or let down the resistance in some way. John just about managed that, but remained convinced that the kidnap of Kreipe was merely a public school game and counter productive.

While John told me his story Gill sat quietly by, but when he went to the bar to order some more beers she said,

It's good he's talking to you like this. He hasn't mentioned these things before. He was genuinely surprised and overwhelmed with his reception in the taxi driver's bar. It's been so good for him.

John came back again and we talked some more. The heroes of my adult life have been the British officers and men who fought with the Greeks against the Germans and now I was talking to one. But the conversation was not easy. One can expect that brave men can be modest and not wish to talk about their past deeds. My father is the same. But John did not seem to have any interest in the war, or his role in it. Many books have been written on this field of operations and its protagonists are still well known.

But John had not read one book on the subject. It was as if, having left Greece in 1945, he had not thought about it until his return a few days earlier. He just got on with his simple life as a salesman for agricultural machinery. Patrick Lee Fermor, one of the main characters from those times, still lived with his cats in the Peloponnese, not far away and I asked John if he would pay him a visit.

No. I won't do that. But, there is one person I would like to see.

There was silence as I waited for him to formulate his question.

I don't suppose you have heard of him but there was a Cretan man, a real hero, whose job was to run between the resistance bands to take messages. His name was George... George

George Psychoundakis.

That's right. How do you know?

So I told him. George Psychoundakis had written a book, *The Cretan Runner*, which told in a simple and dignified way how this shepherd had fought in the resistance. In those days communications were a major problem. Radio sets were heavy, not that portable; their signals could be traced and the roads were under German control. George who, as a shepherd moved his flocks over all the hills and mountains before the war, knew every footpath and trail. His approach was simple. He ran between the bands, sometimes for one or two days, carrying messages and orders. A few years ago he had written his book.

John was very excited about this.

What happened to him? Do you have any idea where he lives? How can I contact him?

So I told him.

The Greeks do not treat their heroes well. Shepherds do not own land, the flocks had gone and after the war George Psychoundakis fell on bad times. He was unemployed, but in his spare time used to tend the graves of the Commonwealth soldiers. He also worked part time in the German cemetery in Heraklion, which is ironic considering that he was responsible for putting some of them there. I went to my room and fetched my copy of the book. The address of the cemetery was printed inside the front cover.

Two days later the pair of them went away. I learnt nothing more about John, not even his surname. I have read all there is about Crete in that period and can find no reference to the man. What I knew then was what I know now. He was a quiet man and a brave man and so modest that he wasn't even aware he was being modest. These people; Cretan, British and German too, were a different generation, they had a different quality. There are not many left.

Death in a Greek Village

Many years ago, when I was new to the village, I had a friend called Manolis, a handsome, friendly man who swam and fished and cooked barbecues on the beach and chased girls. And then his brother Anthonis died and everything changed. I wasn't there at the time, but soon after I returned to the village and tried in my awkward, uncomfortable, European way to say and do the right things. In these circumstances Europeans find it difficult to say what we should and I believe that the reason for this is that we have literally nothing to say. There is nothing we can do. We have lost our rituals; lost the ceremonies that accomplish death and comfort the living. In these circumstances we are helpless. Nevertheless, Manolis and I went out daily in a little rowing boat and sat on beaches in the shade. We took a bottle of ouzo and a litre of water each and we got drunk. We did not talk about death, or guilt, or Anthonis. We did not talk at all. Day after day we just got drunk.

In those days there was no harbour in the village. When the ferry boat came it would stop out at sea and depending on the weather, we would go out in small boats to fetch the passengers and the freight. Even if we went in Niko's boat, at ten metres the biggest in the village, this could be a hazardous operation. Unloading large women and old men and fridges and cookers from the back of a ferry boat at sea is difficult, even in a calm sea with no wind, but with bad weather it can be dangerous. To start with, no captain likes to be close to land when the wind blows onshore and so the ferries would normally meet us way out to sea. The further out we were, the bigger the waves and, even if the captain knew what he was doing, which was not always the case, and turned the ferry to shelter us from the wind, it was difficult. The system was for the captain of the ferry to radio to Nikos in the village and announce its imminent arrival. Nikos would gather whatever outward bound passengers there were, take two or three young men to help, and go out to sea to meet the ferry. It was then up to us to get close enough for the passengers to scramble on board the ferry and for the arrivals to get into Nikos' boat. Villagers, tourists, goats, freezers, washing machines, flour, tools, seeds, cement, vegetables and fruit would pass back and forward. Sometimes things got broke, sometimes they fell overboard, but Nikos is a good captain and although the occasional passenger did fall into the sea nobody was ever hurt and none were lost.

One stormy day, Manolis came to me and asked for help. The ferry boat was coming and was fetching from Athens a marble sarcophagus for Anthonis' grave. He wanted me and some of the boys to help. So off we went with Nikos. There were no passengers, it was too rough and as we got close to the ferry boat we knew there would be problems. Marble is fragile, as well as heavy, and we had to come in beam-side against the lowered car ramp, so that two or three of us could get a grip and lift the pieces of the sarcophagus gently into the boat. The waves were big, say two metres, so big that if we were caught under the ramp as the waves came up, the boat would be crushed and maybe one of us would be injured, or even killed. Time and time again Nikos came in beam-side on, we would unload one or two pieces and then the wind would take us away from the ferry and Nikos would have to go round again. It was difficult, it was dangerous, it took time, but we managed. We broke one piece of the marble, but that didn't matter too much; we were pleased that we could do something for Manolis and the memory of Anthonis. We thought of these things in silence as we returned to the mole and I for one deliberately stood in the spray so that the sea salt mixed with my salty tears. We tied up and silently began to unload the marble and then the women of the family saw what we were doing. They came down to the mole wailing laments for Anthonis and as they wailed they took their black scarves from their heads and scratched their faces and pulled their long, grey hair and tore their clothes. I stood helplessly as Manolis tried to comfort them, but tears filled my eyes as the women wailed and screamed. Suddenly I saw a tourist fumbling for his camera. I walked towards him and I think we both know that if he had taken a picture I would have beaten him badly, maybe killed him before anyone intervened. That moment with those women's voices had affected me so much that I experienced the catharsis and anger of grief as if it had been my son or my brother that had died. I stood there shaking as the tourist turned and walked quickly away.

So why did I have such strong feelings? How does the village way with death differ from the Western experience? Why is it that the Western world is embarrassed by death, but rural Greece is not?

The most obvious difference is that in the village the public display of feeling and the involvement of the community in sharing grief is not just encouraged, it is demanded. Thus when someone in the family, or a close friend, or someone respected in the village dies, then you wear black. The women wear all-black clothes and the men do the same, or at least wear black armbands. There is no music, the men will not sing or dance for a year or more, maybe the women will never dance again. The men grow beards. All these are public manifestations to show feelings and allow the sharing of emotions and of grief. Daily, sometimes two times a day, the women of the deceased will go to the cemetery, quietly, by themselves, without fuss. Look around. Maybe you will see a black figure walking up the hill alone. There in the cemetery she will cry and wail, weeping for her loved one and weeping with other women that may be there, sharing the same purpose. The women share their grief, comfort one another and show that they are doing the right thing.

They sing laments, sometimes modified from traditional songs.

> Oh, Anthonis, Anthonis, why have you left me all alone?
> Why did you leave me and go on a journey?
> Why so soon?
> Why leave me like this?

When someone from the village dies the news spreads fast. Whispers pass from one to another and a silence spreads like a damp mist through the community. The men in the *cafeneion* lower their voices for a while, then go home. Children are called in from play and the village goes to bed early. That night the women of the family and friends will gather outside the house of the deceased crying and singing laments. Other women of the village, special, older women, will undress and wash the body and dress it again in good clothes. Elderly villagers often choose and set aside clothes carefully in anticipation of their last journey. I know of one old man who has had his own grave dug for two years now.

The corpse is laid out in a coffin with a white shroud up to the waist and the eyes are closed. People from the village come to the house, they kiss the forehead of the corpse and give their condolences and the body is watched over through the night. The priest comes and there is silence as he prays for forgiveness of the sins of the deceased. Candles are lit and the laments begin again and we hear the soft, sad, songs rising up through the night.

> Stay here Anthonis, just for tonight.
> Please stay, and leave me in the morning.

In the morning the church bell is rung, *ding ding, ding ding, ding ding*. Intense, public grief is shown as the body is carried from the house and in the church as the priest leads prayers for the purification of the soul and for a swift journey from this life to paradise. *Ding ding, ding ding, ding ding*, the procession winds its way through the village. It halts outside the home of the dead person and villagers come and stand outside their houses as the cortege passes through the village and on up the hill. *Ding ding, ding ding, ding ding*. In the graveyard the ceremony is short. The shroud is pulled over the face of the corpse, the coffin lowered into the ground, there are prayers and close family members throw earth into the grave. In Europe that would be the end of the story, the family and friends would be left alone to get on with their grief on an individual basis. Maybe they would never speak of their grief or even mention the name of the dead person again. They would suffer alone. But here we do things differently. We recognise that both the living and the dead are embarking on a journey. The living follow rituals for comfort and support while the dead are helped on their way to paradise.

After the funeral there is a small gathering at the house of the dead person, *koliva* (a sweet mixture of boiled wheat, cinnamon, nuts and raisins) is handed out and sometimes a simple meal is shared. The next day the house is cleaned and the clothes of the dead person burnt or given away. Three days after the funeral the first memorial service (*mnimosino*) is held. Women gather at the graveside and laments are sung and the priest leads prayers for forgiveness. Later the grave is decorated with flowers, candles are lit, and oil and photographs are left behind.

After forty days something akin to a wake is held in the dead person's house and the family sit quietly in candlelight, with the doors open and talk about the person who has departed. This is a moving and poignant time and important, because only now can the soul of the dead leave the house and leave the familiar places. By behaving correctly and attending to the proper conduct of the various ceremonies, the family ensures that the dead one's soul is released to go to paradise.

> We have a long journey before us
> And a wide river to cross.
> Mother mine, you have left me.
> How do I cross the river alone?

During the forty days villagers have told me that they are visited by the dead relative in the night. Not in a dream, they say, it wasn't a dream . . . my father came to me and he said,

> Thank you for what you have done for me.
> I am happy now.

Another told me that her father came in the night and said,

> Do not trust your brother. He will steal your money.

Gradually, depending on the status of the deceased, or the beliefs of the family, or the social pressures of the village, the dead person is slowly allowed to drift away and the living slowly return to their new life. There are visits to the cemetery, the grave is cleaned, *koliva* is handed out on the proper anniversaries. Sometimes members of the family gather together on the anniversary of the death, but in the main, watched over by the village, the family are left alone to their grief. They and the dead person continue gently on parallel journeys, until five or more years later.

Then the remains are dug up! This may seem a strange or even barbaric, thing to do, but it fits a pattern. From the moment of death it is believed that the soul has begun a journey, a journey that is only complete when the body has decomposed and there are only clean white bones left. The belief is that, as the flesh putrefies, the sins of the flesh are forgiven and thus white bones signify a purified soul. So the remains are exhumed and inspected, to see if all the flesh has decomposed. This is normally the case and then the family can finally say good-bye.

> Don't cry my sweet mother.
> Don't have a heavy heart.
> Our fate has written that we must be parted.
> Go home, mother. Farewell.

The wife, or the daughter, with the help of other women, gather the bones together, maybe cradles the skull, maybe kisses it. The bones are wrapped in white linen, or put in a box and stored in a corner of the graveyard in the ossuary. If the bones are not clean, the soul is thought to be in torment caused by problems in the family or the village. More funeral services are performed, everyone is very sad and mourning begins again.

You are a man. You walk and the pain passes.
I am a woman and the pain remains.
What more can I do? What more do you want?

Another year, or two and the bones are exhumed again until eventually they are declared clean and free of impure flesh and the soul of the dead person cannot return again. It has passed on to paradise.

Put away your black clothes, put away your dirty clothes.
Whenever I set out for home I meet rain and mist,
Whenever I turn back to that foreign land,
I meet sunshine and good roads.

So where does this leave a *xenoi*, a foreigner, in this village? Long ago I learned to observe and not to judge. This does not mean that I remain unaffected. I too feel the anger, the guilt, the loss, and sometimes I can express these feelings and feel the relief from this expression.

But there is something else. I was having a bad time. My mother had died. I was alone, living in a room by the sea at the time, and I thought I was handling myself well, but inside there was anger and depression. I was a troubled man. I woke in the night and found it difficult to go back to sleep. I lay awake and counted down the waves. Ten, nine, eight . ... then, in the room, there was a voice.

Today we are going to meet someone

Nothing like this had ever happened before; no voices, no meeting, nobody. And it didn't feel like a dream. Now, somebody was leading me firmly away. We passed through a small, English country town, familiar from dreams in the distant past, cobbled streets, a bookshop with bow windows and bullseye glass. Left turn up a steep hill and then I am led into a dark room and facing me, sitting up in an armchair, is my mother. Pause for a second and imagine how you would feel to meet someone who had died eighteen months before. Who then says, in a perfectly normal and oh so familiar voice:

Hello, my son. I am sorry to hear that you have been having troubles lately. I think you will find that things will get better now.

Then peace, total peace and relaxation and of course, sleep.

Throughout the world there are many people who believe we can communicate with the dead. Some people are thought to have special skills in that direction. I do not know what happened to me that night. I do not believe in ghosts, but I did meet my mother. Only in my mind of course, but isn't that where we meet people most of the time anyway? Rationally it was only a dream, though a timely one and very different from any dream I have had before. But the funny thing, the really funny thing, is that the old girl was right. Things got better.

So when you see people in black, or women crying, or a small group carrying candles through the village in the dark, when you are handed a small bag of *koliva*, or sweets, by an old lady at Easter time, try not to think it strange. Don't be clever or reach for your camera. Act with courtesy and love and ask yourself what life and death is all about. The people of the village have their way. Is yours better?

The Lesson

In their five metre open boat, hugging the rocks and the cliffs, the outboard motor straining away against the current and against the wind, they butt north. Seen from the mountains they appear tiny and heroic. Two men in a small boat in a vast sea.

Daily they search for food, collect salt from the rocks, look for limpets and cockles, gather edible seaweed and succulent plants from the sea bed and the cliffs and, of course, fish. They fish to eat and to feed their families and to exchange fish for flour and meat and sometimes for money. They fish in any weather and any sea. First farmers and then city dwellers have pushed hunters and gatherers out of Europe. Then, the European Community helped big boats and big companies to destroy the livelihood of people like these. Perhaps these two are the last representatives of the old way, of an old people who lived not by changing, but by understanding their environment. When they have gone, a people will have gone and a knowledge too. If this seems an easy life, just look at their hands, just look at their faces. If someone asks

Was the sea rough today?

Just listen to their bitter laughter. They do not think of these things, just point the prow of the boat into the wind so that they do not get wet from the spray. It is, as always, windy and there is a strong current, but the waves are not big.

Everything in the sea is ours, my friend.
From the young man.
Everything.

He has seen something, the young one; a spec of flotsam rising and falling, sometimes visible, sometimes not. It is two hundred metres ahead, across the straits between the two islands, where the sea is rough. The wind has changed now, coming east between the islands, so they have to turn west into it. A classic manoeuvre; point into the wind, keep dry and keep snug to the lee shore. Safe and dry. Soon they turn about, slowly enter the rough water with the wind from the stern quarter, *prima* it is called here, and they edge closer to Saria until they are safe and they don't get wet.

Well done. From the old man, as they get closer to the spec. Lets have a look

The object is white, a container of sorts. Worth having, but when the get close they can see it is a float attached to a long fishing line, a *paragadi*. It is not flotsam. It belongs to someone.

Leave it. The old man again.

No. Says the young one, It's those bastards from Kalymnos. We have to work fast. Pull in the line.

The old man did not like this; it was stealing. He looked around. They worked hard and fast, pulling in the *paragadi*, unhooking fish, pulling in more line. They greedily grabbed fish.

Fishing boat.
Where?
There, to the north.

They could see the fishing boat; two, maybe three kilometres away. They had been seen. Quickly they let out the line they had taken into their boat, hid the fish they had stolen and continue their journey. The fishing boat disappeared behind the headland to the north, but they would have to meet it soon.

What do we say?

The young man. Silence for a while as the old one thinks.

We tell them we were fishing with *syrti* (a lure) for tuna, we caught a fish, but it went deep and our line was caught in theirs. The tuna got away and we had to cut our line.

The old man was angry now. He did not like to lie.

Fuck Kalymnos.

They head north, close to the coast, out of the wind, chugging from the shelter of one rock to the shelter of the next, from the safety of one small bay to the safety of the next; Mairia, Asproas, Palatia. They come closer to the large fishing boat. It is a wooden *caique*, blue and white, clean and in perfect order. Two hundred metres now and they see with dismay that it is not from Kalymnos, but from Forni. The crew are three brothers. Nice guys, good guys, friends. They have made a big mistake, really screwed things up this time.

Shit! From the old man. You talk. But careful. One of them has binoculars round his neck. For sure they saw us.

So the young man talks and explains about the mythical *syrti* and explains that they had caught a tuna, but it had dived deep and tangled their line with that of the *paragadi*. The fish had gone and they could not untangle the *syrti* so they had cut their line so as not to destroy the paragadi. He asks them to look out for their *syrti* when they picked up the *paragadi*.

The men from Forni speak slowly and softly. They would pick up their *paragadi* soon and agree to look out for the broken *syrti*. They do not smile, they are very serious.

They don't believe us, the old man says, as they move away.

Maybe.

They continue north round the tip of Saria where the sea is rough and the fish are big. They are going diving. Diving in this part of the world means spear fishing. You need 5 mm-thick rubber suits, goggles, flippers, weights to counteract the buoyancy of the rubber suit and good lungs. Bottled air is forbidden. You also need a very visible balloon. This you pull along behind as you swim, to warn boats of your presence, so their propellers don't hack off your fingers or toes, or their keels smash your skull. You anchor your boat close to the coast, you kit up and you dive. Good guys, and the younger of the two was very, very good, can dive up to about 30 metres. It is dark at this depth and to shoot fish you have to enter into a cave, sometimes several metres into a cave, lit only by a hand held torch. Sometimes you have to squeeze into a cave, or swim into a side branch, or both. This may sound dangerous. It is dangerous. If you have good lungs, and the young man has good lungs, you can stay down and work for up to two minutes at a time and you do this all day. Up, down. Up, down. Hour after hour.

The secret to successful diving is to stay calm. If you don't, especially if you panic, the heart beats faster and you use up oxygen. The less oxygen you use the longer you stay down and the more fish you get to see and the more you shoot. Simple really. Try it sometime. These two were used to working together for five or six hours at a stretch. The young man was by far the better of the two divers, but between them they could catch up to 20 kg of fish a day and sponges and octopus and maybe a crayfish on top of that. If they caught fish they lived well.

The sea is choppy, not dangerous, but wild and difficult to fish. They work in parallel, the young man further out to sea, diving deep for prime fish and the old one working the rocky edge as it plunges down, sheer, from the cliffs above.

The trick for him is to spot fish ahead and dive deeper than they are, say five to ten metres, then drive the fish up and shoot them from below. The sea is very clear, but as the waves hit the cliff and the rocks it explodes into brilliant white bubbles, a sunburst of energy hiding the fish and obscuring fissures in the rocks. The old man is wary; once or twice he is thrown into the rocks and he doesn't want to have his arms or legs caught between them as the waves subside. That would be painful. That would be dangerous. He doesn't want his face mashed up any more either, nor does he fancy rubbing his hands or face on the sharp, black spines of the sea urchins that are so abundant here. So, he is very, very careful.

The sea is the enemy, his old father used to say. The sea is the enemy.

The system is to shoot fish, thread them onto a line attached to your balloon and swim on. The technique is to concentrate, be efficient, be alert, work hard. After two or more hours they return to the boat, sit for a while as they release the shot fish from their lines into the bottom of the boat and discuss their next move. They decide to go back south where the sea is not so rough and dive again.

Diving is hard work, not just physically hard, but mentally exhausting too. If you are 30 metres under the water with 20 seconds of air left in your lungs, you concentrate hard. Especially in the dark, in a cave with a valuable fish in front of you. A mistake could lose you the fish, or your life. You don't want to lose either. Diving can also be relaxing. The thrill of the hunt, the necessity to breathe deeply and regularly, the incredible variety of life, means that diving is like a drug, an addictive, but natural, recreational drug. Above all it is the colours that impress. Even the dullest of fish has bright colours underwater, even the darkest of plants weaves a pattern so stunning and mesmeric that you want to go on and on, deeper and deeper. Seaweed changes colour with the seasons, sometimes dark brown, sometimes fresh green. In the autumn you get purple flowers on dark brown leaves, or violet mixed with orange. A Paris couturier would be applauded for such an outrageous mix.

The sea never keeps still and our two divers move with it, up and down, side to side, as the waves take them and from north to south as the current moves, so that they swim to stay still. They dive again and again, try to relax, try to save energy They don't swim down, but glide, letting gravity and the weights do the work, but swim up, breath gone, strength gone, on the edge of panic.

Hours pass and the sun begins to set. They are exhausted as they return to their boat, haul themselves in and prepare to head back to the village. Saying nothing, the one nearest the engine pulls in the anchor and takes the helm. Steering the boat to avoid the waves he keeps close to the rocks, always heading into the wind. The other one prepares the lure and they fish as they head south. At the same time they get out of their wet suits, get dried and get dressed without dropping their clothes into the water, fish and blood slopping about all over the bottom of the boat. Snot streams down their faces, their arms are sore, their hands cut and their bodies ache. They are burnt by the sun and cold in the wind. They have worked hard, but don't have many fish. They see the Forni boat again. They have to pass close by.

Ask about the *syrti*, the old one says, or they will be suspicious.

Cautiously they go close.

Iassu.

Iassu

How was your luck?

Not bad, and you.

Not bad.

Did you find our *syrti*?
Yes
What?
Yes, we found it. Come over this side.

Frantic thoughts. They know there was no *syrti*, they know we were stealing their fish. Panic. But don't show it.

But they cannot say no. They have to steer their little boat to the land side of the *caique*; they will have to pass under two or three ropes mooring it to the rocks. They will be trapped. They are only two in a small boat, the guys from Forni are three and the *caique* towers over them. And they are armed. All fishermen in this part of the world have guns on board. The Forni guys will be angry.

But they cannot say no, so they edge around, tense, nervous, spear guns close to hand.

Here is your *syrti*, says one of the brothers. Give me a plastic bag.

Confused, they stand up in their boat to see and hand over a bag for the found *syrti* that had not been lost.

One of the brothers picks up a prime, pink, bream. A fine fish. He puts it into the bag and another and another and more. Altogether, maybe three or four kilos. They watch tense and confused, ready for some one to say something, prepared for some attack. But the attack does not come.

The brother hands over the bag.

Here, take these. Better than some old *syrti*.

They relax, they are ashamed. The guys from Forni know, but are not going to say anything. They are good men. Kind men. Proper men.

Thank you, with humility from them both, thank you.

They pass under two ropes and outside the anchor rope. They pull away from the *caique*.

Bye and good luck.
To the next time.

They head south. They let out the lure. They are silent. For a long time they are silent. They pull the lure, but no fish takes the *syrti*, no tuna, no barracuda, no *maiatico*, no *palamida*. Nothing. They kept in close to the cliffs, between the rocks, out of the wind. They say nothing; each alone in their small boat, the cry of Eleanora falcons coming from the dark over their heads.

After a while, the old man, as if to himself,

Everything in the sea is ours.

From the young man, nothing.

Ballanos

Ballanos is dying. He lies in bed in Rhodes hospital, his great long frame reaching from end to end of the bed and he is dying. His huge feet, great mounds in the bed, are hidden, but his big hands are stretched out to see on clean, white sheets. His length is there. His great bulk is gone.

My bones will not see home again, his visitors hear, but pretend not to.

The earth of Rhodes will cover them. I will not go home again

The nurses know he is someone, someone important, but they are young and from a different island. They do not know who this giant is, or what he had been.

Ballanos was born in 1910, born under Turkish rule. He could not remember the Turks, but I have heard men and women even older then him talk about the *effendi* and men in baggy, black trousers. In 1912 the Dodecanese became Italian, according to some decision taken by great powers to the north, arrogantly deciding the futures of small nations.

The Italians were not despotic rulers; they liked the island. They liked the girls and the music and the food. Like all colonialists they tried to impose their own language and indeed, much to the surprise of uninformed tourists, all of the old people still speak some Italian. They even tried to stop the teaching of Greek, but were outsmarted. The people just took their schools and classes elsewhere and priests would visit each child every week at night time to teach Greek language and Greek history. This game and others developed over the years. Taxes were collected and not collected, sheep and goats were counted and not counted and a balance of coexistence achieved. Until *ochi* day that is. The great powers were at war again. Britain, France and Germany at first, then, as France was about to fall, Mussolini declared war on Britain, invaded France and gave an ultimatum to the Greeks. Allow our armies free access to Greece, was the demand. *Ochi* (No!), the response from all sections of Greek society and from all Greeks everywhere. So on 28 October 1940 they were at war, Italy and Greece, the battleground being Albania and the mountains of northern Greece. A twentieth century, motorised army, steeled by campaigns in Abyssinia, Spain and Libya, against a rag, tag and bobtail collection of working class volunteers and upper class officers. The people, men, women, children, came to fight the Italians in the mountains in the snow and the people won. The Italians were repulsed, Mussolini embarrassed, and it was left to the Germans to invade Greece.

It was strange to be in the village at the time, under Italian rule, technically Italian citizens, but Greek to the heart and to the bone. There could have been an uprising, but they were unarmed and it would be futile. Besides they had nothing personally against these Italians; some were now their brothers or sons in law. So the young men decided to go to the mainland, to volunteer to fight the Italians and later the Germans. They first joined the army and later became *andartes*, freedom fighters. Technically they were committing treason by leaving to fight the Italians. If caught and identified they would be shot, so they slipped away in the dark in ones and twos; a small boat here, a little ship there, a fishing boat if it was Greek. How many men do you think left this little village to go far away to fight for freedom? Five, ten, twenty maybe? Sixty-three stole away. Sixty-three, Ballanos among them, the core of a new generation. Some did not come back, others came after many years.

Ballanos returned after more than twenty years. If you are six foot four, seventeen stone and have size fourteen boots you cannot sneak back into a small village unnoticed, but he was quiet and it took many years before the story could be told, for this was a time of repression, of the right wing and the Colonels.

When I knew him he was well into his eighties, still big and immensely strong. He had a small, but heavy, wooden boat with an old outboard motor. When he returned from fishing he would not anchor his boat, but rather pull it up onto the beach with the assistance of any old colleague, or, if necessary, pull it up the beach by himself. No other man in the village, no matter their age, could do that. Being a cautious man and trusting nobody, he would take off the outboard motor, lift its thirty kilo weight onto his shoulder and take it home. He lived over half a kilometre away, up hill and he did not stop. Could you do that at eighty-eight years old? Could you do that now?

For some reason Ballanos liked me and sitting in the *cafeneion*, told me some of his tales. Simple ones, like meeting a British army officer liaising with ELAS the Greek resistance army of the mainland. This man also had big feet and gave a pair of boots to Ballanos, a precious gift for this giant fighting in the mountains. He also told me of the *andartes* meeting in a mountain town, towards the end, when the Germans were nearly defeated.

There were ten thousand of us, he said and Aris (the commander) came on a white horse and talked to us.

Later I found a picture of this occasion in a book on ELAS. A man on a white horse, surrounded by fierce men with beards and women wearing bandoliers and waving guns in the air. I showed the picture to Ballanos who looked at it for a long time, closely, with one eye, through his bottle thick glasses.

That's him, he said, Aris, on a white horse.

Ballanos was proud to be in a book and I was proud to show him.

He was in many battles and one is still talked about in the village. It was to be an ambush. A hot, hot afternoon, Ballanos and two others, hid behind rocks, waiting for a German truck. Because he could carry it, he had the machine gun. Six hours they waited, silent, not daring to shit, or speak, or smoke, watching the road and watching the crest behind. Looking for grey helmets, looking for signs of betrayal, fearful that they too were being ambushed. Then, *grrrr grrrr* as the truck, loaded with SS troops, came slowly on and up the hill. *Grrr grrr grrrr*, it came closer, closer. Ballanos stood. He fired. *Bam, bam, bam, bambambam, bambambambambam.* Bodies, blood, stones, teeth, hair, skull, steel, petrol sprayed everywhere. Then silence. Tick, tick, tick, drip, drip. No movement. Nothing. They relaxed. They looked at one another. Walked slowly to the wrecked truck. Suddenly a sound. A German soldier leaps from the back of the truck, hobnails crunching on the stone track. Ballanos fired, or rather didn't. Overheated, the machine gun had jammed. So they laughed as this one escaped, throwing away his rifle, scuttling and slithering back down the hill.

I got twelve, he told me, could have been thirteen.

Then he stood up to give his seat to a tourist. A German as it happened.

When the Germans were defeated the civil war came. Being a communist, Ballanos was on the losing side. He was captured, beaten, imprisoned and exiled. He lost an eye. They nearly killed him. Ballanos was calm about these things. He accepted them. They happened to hundreds of thousands of Greeks; abandoned by Stalin and defeated by the right wing and the British and the Americans, scattered through Russia and the Balkans. The Great powers, once again deciding the future of Greece and the Greeks. What hurt was the pension. Ballanos fought the Italians and then the Germans for six hard years. He fought in the mountains and the plains, in ice and snow, in hot burning sun. He fought with bullets and bayonets, with fists, with rocks, with grenades. But because he had been with ELAS these years were not counted. Those who sat on their arses, those who ran away, even those who collaborated, were given their pensions. Those who fought were not given what was their right. And this hurt. He didn't say much when he returned. He got by with his goats, his bees and his fishing. He didn't say much, but inside he hurt.

And now this Greek hero is dying. The nurses look through the window. He lies there still, one hand moves slightly, his eyelids flicker. Never to see home again. Never. For a moment his body stiffens, arms by his side. For a second he is to attention, his hand quivers, then, nothing. Ballanos is dead.

We forget too soon you and I. We do not honour our heroes. We forget the sacrifices they made so that we could live in happiness. Of the sixty-three who left the village to fight, only five are left.

And Ballanos is dead.

Emetis from Embola

The oral traditions of small communities are vital for the transmission and preservation of local culture and history. They pass on from generation to generation those stories that are too minor ever to appear in print, but which are, nevertheless, important to the life of distinct cultures. Story telling keeps alive family and village characters, language, dialect and traditions. Sometimes, the village opens up to deliver its secrets and idiosyncratic proverbs and sayings lead to intriguing stories.

When you ask people in the village where they are going, or where they have been, they might say, with a smile

I am going to Embola.

or

I am coming from Embola.

or even

I am Emetis from Embola.

As told to me, the origin of these sayings started around 1700. A local man from Olymbos wanted some good wood to build a door frame for his house. In those days, one way to find wood was to look for flotsam thrown up by the sea on the beaches of Saria. Even today, when there has been a Sirocco or southern wind, I go to look on Alimounda beach, the other side of Palatia in North Saria.

So, the Olymbitis took his boat and went to Alimounda. There he found wood, but something else too, a man, naked and frightened. I was told he was *Arabis* or black, but I suspect he was an Egyptian or Turk. The man hid, but the Olymbitis tried to help him. The dress of Olymbitic men in those days used to include long undergarments and, over them, what are called *braches*, or baggy trousers. The English word breeches clearly has the same root. So the Olymbitis took off his *braches* and laid them out for the naked man. Encouraged by this friendly gesture the *Arabis* came closer and put on the *braches*. The Olymbitis shared his food with the shipwrecked man and together they returned to Olymbos. They had no words in common, but the *Arabis* told his story in mime and gesture. He had been on a ship that had sunk and he was the only survivor. He had been shipwrecked and stranded in Alimounda for thirty days, taking water from the spring and eating berries, roots and honey.

Over a period of time the grateful *Arabis* worked for the Olymbitis and paid him back for the rescue. The local people called him Mohammed, or, in the local dialect, Emetis. Eventually Mohammed moved away from Olymbos to an area called Embola, not far from Avlona. He stayed there seven years, planting and growing produce and even keeping animals. He learnt a little Greek and when he met someone he would say he was Emetis from Embola. He and the Olymbitis remained close friends. Then, in the seventh year, looking out from one of the shepherd's huts that are still found on the ridge above Vananda, he saw a ship whose flag he recognised. The ship was anchored in the bay to take in fresh water. Emetis ran down the paved donkey track shouting and screaming. The strangers recognised the greetings, welcomed Mohammed, heard his story and when they left the island Mohammed went with them. The people from the village knew what had happened and were pleased that Emetis had found some of his own people.

Now, our friend the Olymbitis was a pious man and wanted to build a chapel on some land of his at Tristomo. He was a poor man and working on his own, in his spare time, this project took several years. Unfortunately for the Olymbitis, these years coincided with increased authority and control by the Turks over the island. They found out that he had built a church and had done so without permission. They seized him, put him in chains, and sent him away to Constantinopolis. Alimounda was the furthest the Olymbitis had been in all his life, so to be sent in chains to court in Constantinople was terrifying . The city was a mixture of Greeks, Turks, Syrians, Egyptians, Africans, Europeans, freemen and slaves, but the rulers were Turks and the language used in prison and in the legal system was Turkish.

The Olymbitis was petrified. Thrown into a stinking, crowded cell, a night without sleep, a babble of barbarian languages, and now he was led in chains through the streets to the courthouse. Down again underground, a dank, dark hole smelling of fear and piss. A name is called, a prisoner led out, time passes, another name, another wretch. Then, as in a dream, his name, but the voice seems friendly and familiar. Someone talks to him in a half remembered dialect, stuttering, stumbling, smiling, a face in bright sunlight suddenly comes into focus.

It is me. Emetis from Embola.

Emetis! Emetis! *Ti kaneis edw*? What are you doing here?

I am the secretary to the court. I am the boss.

They talk and they talk and they talk, bone crushing hugs, arms wildly waving, their raised voices attract the attention of the other court officials. Eventually an explanation is made and some understanding reached between the two comrades. The Turkish legal system was not known for its clemency, but it did have a certain flexibility and, while Mohammed was not exactly the boss, he certainly had influence. He went off to see what could be done. On his return the Olymbitis was a free man.

It was two or three weeks before the Olymbitis made his way back to the village and told his tale. The story was a sensation and soon everyone was saying

I am Emetis from Embola.
Three hundred years later they still are.

The Mule

Crowds of tourists gather here two times a day. They come off the tourist boat, they mill around, they have labels, FCUK, DandG, DKNY, but their labels don't help, they are lost. Someone, a Swede, or a German, gathers them up, puts them on a bus and off they go to another village in the mountains for an authentic experience. In the evening they return with their authentic souvenirs and their authentic memories. Now they sit on the beach, impatient for the boat to leave, or they sit in the bar with foaming beers and bottles of retsina.

Only a few things from our village seem to interest them: our women in their traditional clothes, our animals and fish. They get very excited to see women baking bread outside in the ovens and, when a fishing boat comes in, they gather around in a mob to watch fish being cleaned and scaled. Maybe it is strange to them that food does not come frozen in packets and, for sure, the preparation of an octopus is a total mystery. Whenever I have an octopus and am beating it on a rock, to soften the meat and make it easier to cook, I am surrounded by the babble of foreigners. They keep their distance so as not to be splashed by the ink and they snap with their Nikons and they video with their Sonys, stealing memories, frozen like their food, for the folks back home.

Why is he doing that? An Italian asked Giorgos.

He doesn't like octopus.

I think she believed him.

Sometimes, in all this throng, one of our people will appear, perhaps with a mother goat with two kids on the end of some string, or maybe a donkey loaded with flowers and plants for the goats or wood for the oven. Out come the cameras again and the videos whirl to record the rarest of things, a domesticated animal in a rural village.

The fuss is so much that we hesitate now. We talk about living on a reservation and time our activities to avoid commotion. The women stay inside when the tourists are here; they bake bread in the early morning or in the evenings. We don't bring animals into the village when it is crowded and we clean fish when they have gone. Thus Michaelis, we call him Michaelidis because he is small, has been waiting for the bus to leave. Then he comes down the hill with a baby goat in tow. At eighty-eight years old he is more sprightly than the kid. I watch him as he takes the little animal to the end of the mole and then, without hesitation, throws it into the sea. The kid surfaces, looking a little surprised, and swims back to the beach. I am surprised too and totally perplexed as Michaeli goes to the kiosk, buys a bottle of soda and feeds it to the little goat.

What are you doing? I ask him

He's not well. He tells me. He won't eat.

I ask no more questions.

Generally we love our animals here. We may eat them, we certainly use them, but we look after them. A happy animal is a useful animal; one that is well fed is tasty. We love our animals and care for them like you love your cars and wash and polish them on a Sunday morning. If you have a mule, for example, it may live for twenty years. It may be in a stable next to your room. At night you will hear it feed and hear it sneeze or fart and it will hear you too. So be a little careful; show some respect. Such a mule will have a name, may have carried you on its back when you were a little child, may have known your mother, or your grandfather. And you will work with it twelve or fourteen hours a day. You will talk to it, coax it, curse it, share your secrets, put your arm around it. We have land where there are no roads, so we still need mules and donkeys. We take them in the backs of trucks to the end of the road and we walk with them or ride them from there. Sometimes we take them by boat, but that's another story.

Some animals are remembered long after their death. One such, Jenny, is still talked about today. This mule belonged to a friend of mine, Maroukla, an old lady now. We are not too sure of her age, but she is well over eighty. She bakes bread in the oven outside my window sometimes. Then wood smoke fills my room in the evening, or at night, and I hear her laughing and cackling with the other women. In the morning, on my steps, a fresh, crusty, still warm, loaf. Her thick accent, no d's, no t's, no l's, but with lots of n's is difficult to follow. A donkey, *gaidaros*, is pronounced *garro*, a table, *trapeza* is *trapenzi*. She is not easy to understand, but she is very interesting and one day she told me this story.

In 1944 Maroukla lived with her old parents in a little house on the edge of the village. In the stable they kept their prized mule, some goats and chickens. Each day, when there was work to be done on their land, she walked the mule on the old track on the edge of the cliff, by the sea. If you look, you will find it today. In the evening they would walk back; the mule loaded with leaves and branches and grass, food for the goats. She loved her mule; she had known it all her life and she was proud as she returned home. The war was still on, but most of the Italians had left. And then the Germans came.

It is generally forgotten by historians and social commentators that the Wermacht was not fully mechanised. At the battle of Stalingrad, for example, hundreds of thousands of horses were used. Some were used to transport men and weapons, others to carry fodder, and those that carried fodder themselves needed fodder. For this reason, on the Eastern Front, a scorched earth policy was legitimate and deadly. Many of these beasts of burden were killed, some were eaten. In the Balkans, the need of the German army was for mules as transport animals, to help fight the *andartes* in the mountains of Crete and the mainland. When the Germans first came to the village they went to every house and took a census of the people and of the animals. They counted the goats and sheep, the mules and the donkeys and they took the names of all the people. Later they returned to each house and left a piece of paper in Italian and in Greek. This paper explained that the army wanted mules and that everyone with a mule had to take it to Pigadia in the south. If they disobeyed they would be punished. Each paper had a number on it, a number that identified their house.

The people were dismayed. It was near to the olive harvest and they needed their animals. Besides, they loved them and did not want them used in the mountains against the resistance, but they had to go. In those days there was no road to the south, just donkey tracks, paved in parts. These tracks were hundreds of years old; some built by the Dorians, some maybe dating back to Minoan times. These days young tourists walk them and are proud when they arrive in our village. We welcome them when they arrive. *Bravo*, we say, *Bravo*.

But Maroukla did not feel brave, as she set off before dawn. Her parents were too old to make this forty-kilometre journey; each step was difficult for her. Walking beside this handsome animal, her heart was pain. Inside she cried. Jenny, the mule, seemed to understand there was a problem. Whenever they stopped for a rest or food or for water, it would stand a little too close to her, touch her gently with its nose. She would put her arm round its neck, smell the mule smell in its mane, lean her forehead against its cheek. It took all day to get close to Pigadia. A hot, painful, difficult day. They slept in the hills outside the little town and in the morning went slowly down to meet their fate.

They arrived in the mid-morning. They went to the courthouse built by the Italians. Maroukla tied up her mule with all the others and joined the queue. There were people from the village that she knew, people from other villages, people from all over the island. Even in those days our women were the only ones to keep the old ways, wear the old clothes. So, many people stared at Maroukla and the other women from here. She did not mind. Dressed in black, with her hood drawn tight and the veil across her face, she took refuge inside her clothes. A soldier took her paper, stamped it two times and explained what she had to do. She was to take the mule behind the building and walk round and round the courtyard with the other villagers and their animals. The army would choose the best animals and that would be it. Goodbye. She went slowly outside, unhitched the mule, kissed its neck, smelt that smell and holding her head high, led it round to the courtyard. Two officers were there, cavalry officers, grey uniform, black leather boots, black leather riding crops. They pointed and Maroukla, pulling Jenny, joined the circle. Round and round they went in the hot sun. Round and round, trampling on straw and shit, breathing dust and flies as the officers looked on. This would not last long Maroukla thought. Her mule was one of the best, then this would be over and she would go home alone.

Half an hour went by. Round and round. Round and round. Sometimes they were stopped; an officer would point and a poor, sad villager would lead their mule to the German stables, leave it there and go home. Round and round, round and round. Sad steps, looking down at the ground, the shit, the straw. Maroukla could not understand; her mule was a fine beast. Round and round, only three left; the other two being old, beaten, moth eaten, scrawny things. Ten more minutes, then they were told their mules were useless. Take your papers, take your mules and go. She didn't understand, she looked back to say something to Jenny and saw. She saw that Jenny, her smart, intelligent, handsome mule, was limping a great exaggerated limp. She nearly laughed. She felt weak. Thank god for the veil.

The way Maroukla tells it now, the mule limped to the edge of town and then suddenly they were off, flying over the paths and tracks, flying home to the village, to the fields, the olives, the house, the stable. She cackles, she laughs, she cuts me a *kommati* (little slice) of bread, about six inches thick. Her eyes shine. She hops from one leg to the other. Help me with this load, she says, and I struggle to lift the five huge loaves. She scolds me for being a pathetic man, laughs again and balancing the load on her head she is off along the sea front, round the corner and gone.

I return to my little room. It smells of wood smoke. I sit on my balcony and listen to the music of the sea. I see the red light on the harbour wall and the silhouette of the mountains against the night sky. I sit till it is dark. I hear voices of women and the call of a kestrel, hunting by the light of the sea. Time passes. I am far away.

Mosaic

It is possible, perhaps, to convey some of the larger themes of the village by telling stories, but in truth it is the little things that count; the asides, the scents, the memories, the laughs. These are difficult to capture, impossible to describe. Village life is a mosaic of experiences, a constant barrage of the senses. You can try to understand the world by going everywhere, seeing everything, or you can sit here and learn from what is going on around you. The world is here. Open your eyes, you will see.

The tourist boats come. The men sit in the *cafeneion* to look at the girls; the women are around to keep an eye on the men. In the evening old ladies wait for the tourist boats to go, so that they can come down to the sea and stand with their gnarled feet in the blessed, cool water. They roll up their long dresses, stand in their bloomers and paddle like young children. This is the daily rhythm of the village.

Then there is the blessed Olga; fat, dishevelled, a gargoyle grin trying to attract tourists off the boats to her scruffy restaurant;

Coffee, ice tea, french (fresh) orange juicy, ladies (lentil) soup.

Do you have fish? They ask

Baby (maybe) tomorrow.

Seven nice day.

They wander past, not understanding a word she has said. They stand around the painted menu. Rise pudding is, perhaps, understandable if you are English, but stuffed tom is hardly appetising when you think about it.

There used to be a time when the village was replete with hand painted signs. Some are still there, faded and hard to read. My favourite was:

> Nice rooms with toilet in garden two hundred metres away.

Later, as the level of literacy and perhaps plumbing improved this became;

> Nice rooms with bathroom in garden two hundred metres away

We have more varieties of flowers in Greece than in the whole of Northern Europe. They look beautiful, scattered about the fields, and, when the people go out to cut grass and *horta* and food for their goats, they cut flowers too. A friend of mine, a women who has been coming to the village for many years, saw some beautiful flowers in a bundle of hay being carried back to the village on the back of a donkey.

Those are beautiful, she said. What do you call them?

The old couple with the donkey hold my friend in high regard. They discussed, they thought, they discussed again. Then the old man spoke, slowly and carefully, so my friend could understand.

We call that goat food. He said.

They went on their way, happy to have been of assistance.

There is, too, a wonderful story of Niko, tired after transferring nearly 100 tourists from the ferry boat to the port, being assailed by an irate Italian.

Where is ma' luggage?

What?

Ma' luggage? You ma' luggage?

Don't call me *malakas* (wanker).

Georgos is a handsome young man who loves fish and fishing. A young girl tourist, frustrated by his lack of interest asked him,

Do you prefer fishing or sex?

After a while a puzzled Georgos replied;

Fishing is sex.

Next day she left the village.

In the corner of the beach, every evening in the summer, for their health, a group of old ladies gather, undress from their long black dresses and long white underclothes to reveal swimming costumes. Then, laughing and giggling, helping one another, sometimes with the aid of walking sticks, they slide into the water to swim. At the same time, a group of three men heads off in the other direction, walking to the end of the harbour some twenty minutes away. They do this every night, a combined age of more than 250 years, for their health. They intend to live for ever these people and I wish them well.

One time I drove up to Avlona with a friend of mine to help gather food for the goats. I say help, but his wife did all the work. As we finished and the little harvest was gathered in, a very, very old lady, bent and black, went past.

How's your mother? my friend asked.

Not bad. She said. Not bad, for her age.

An old man, interviewed in our local paper about his life. He was ninety-eight years old, had been in revolutions, uprising and wars, lived in Iraq, Iran, Turkey, America. At the end of the interview they asked.

Do you have any regrets?

He thought for a while.

Yes, he said. I have had a good life. My back is good, my arms are strong, But my knees hurt so I am of no use to anyone. That's what I regret. I can't work anymore.

The women, sitting outside, talk to one another across the village, without seeming to raise their voices. That way, we all know what's going on, we have our own internet. One time the phone rang in my little house. It was Anna from the *cafeneion* 80 metres away.

Put down the phone, she said, and go outside.

Outside she continued the conversation by shouting her news to me.

That night when I was having an ouzo I asked why she did this.

It's cheaper, she said.

Appropriate technology?

Baking bread, a communal effort, gathering the wood, lighting the fire. Smoke swirls through the village, the women come with their bowls of dough, working together, the smell of wood smoke, the smell of fresh bread, the gossip, the laughs. A large chunk of bread, still warm, carefully wrapped in brown paper and placed on the stairs inside my door. Thank you Anna.

Vasillis leaning against the door of his bar, lazily scratching his back on the doorpost. One of the customers looks up.

My donkey does that, he says.

Everyone laughs. Vasillis smiles. Continues scratching his back.

It is a warm night in November, but the Sirocco has come. There is a full moon and the boys are sitting in the yard in Anna's, playing cards and watching the sea. A big wave comes and water, stones, spume and foam swirl inside. They lift up their feet, hold onto their ouzos and carry on playing cards. One of the boys has lost his sayonaras, that wonderful name for what you call flip flops. The next wave brings them back. He grabs them, puts them on the wall to dry, carries on playing. Meanwhile, by the oven, a group of men gather the flotsam and jetsam that the Sirocco always brings. This is fun, but they are a little worried as the waves are now coming over the harbour wall and if their boats are not anchored well they are in danger. They dash to gather their harvest before the sea takes it back — plastic bottles, cans, a chair, bits of wood. They get their shoes and trouser legs wet, but it's fun. Kanakis, as always, is at the forefront.

There is some good plywood here, he shouts, above the sound of the sea, the same colour as my boat. There is a pause, as he looks closer.

Shit. It is my boat

Poor Kanakis, the eternal hippy, had not anchored properly. The boat's a dead loss, but nice plywood.

Antonis came to make a presentation to the village council last summer. He is an engineer, a sophisticated man from Rhodes, and he has some proposals concerning the water system. He came in his boat on a calm day, with the idea of staying a few days and doing some fishing. Being smart, he had a pre-meeting with some council members. They drink wine and ouzos. Everyone went home for the siesta, but it was hot, too hot, in his boat so Antonis curled up by the sea under the little concrete bridge by the rocks. He slept well. When he awoke, his shoes were gone, washed off his feet by the wake from the ferry boat. He did not have a spare pair. He made the presentation to the full council that evening in Olymbos. Barefoot. Nobody seemed to mind. He got the contract.

I think this story is true. If not, then it should be. An Italian film producer had the idea for *Mediterraneo,* a film about a band of Italian soldiers whiling away the war in a sleepy Greek village. They had a good script, a fine cast and enough money. All that was required was to shoot the film.

Their research was thorough; they spent months looking at maps and reading articles, talking to friends and travel agents. Eventually they settled on Diafani. They rang Nikos. Yes, there is room in my hotel. Yes, you can come here to make your film. We are waiting to welcome you.

The film crew come. It is autumn, quiet, sleepy. The Italians discover Tristomo. That's the place; the crew will do it up, paint the old houses white, go there every day in Nikos' boat. But they are loud, demanding, self centred, unsympathetic to the local people.

How much?

For what?

Your boat

It's not for sale.

For rent?

It's not for rent.

We will pay well.

I cannot.

Why not?

I have to take the people to Saria. It is the olive season. The women are old. They cannot stay there at night. I have to go there and back every day.

But we will make Diafani famous.

No

We will make you rich.

No

We will put you in the film

No

So the Italians who wanted to make a film about a sleepy, backward Greek village had to leave. Diafani was too sleepy, too backward. That's what they thought anyway. They made the film on Kastellorizo and started a mini tourist boom there, Diafani missed out. It's not a bad film and I am pleased for Kastellorizo. I am even more pleased for Diafani.

Minas walking slowly towards me on his stumpy, arthritic legs, clutching something in his hands. Minas, the carpenter, who treats me like the golden goose, demanding a radio here, a Black and Decker drill there. Minas, my adopted father, stands before me, looks at me through his thick glasses and hands me an intricate Diafani knot of beautifully carved hardwood. Suspicious and fearful of being overcharged, I ask

What's this?

It's for you. It took three days to make.

And?

It's a present for you.

Why?

Because I love you.

And he walks away slowly, rocking on his painful legs.

I stand there clutching my gift. A humbled man.

But it's the women, always the women, sitting alone or in groups, sitting on stairs in the evening, or on flat roofs, sitting by the sea, staying cool, gossiping, catching the news of the day. Look around when the ferry boat comes. They will be there, in the dark at night, or in the shade in the day, sitting quietly, their black scarves covering their faces, watching the harbour. They look to see who has come with who, or who has left their husband or their wife at home in America, or Rhodes, or Piraeus. They talk quietly to one another. Look how much luggage they have. How big the grandchildren have grown. Isn't she fat, hasn't he got old? Is that a new washing machine? Their other one is only a year old.

They sit there quietly too, thinking of children who have gone away, grandchildren they will never see. When the ferry boat has gone they will be there still; quiet, with scarves over their faces, resolute, reassuring. The women of the village.

The Woman at the Cemetery

Cemeteries on our islands nearly always overlook the sea. I do not know why this is, but feel it is not to do with Christianity. It seems natural to me that the bones of an island people should be laid to rest overlooking the sea. The cemetery in our village is no exception. You go up the hill, past the old church, through the trees and there you are. It is steep up the hill and we joke that for your last journey you are lucky that you do not have to walk. But it is difficult to carry a coffin up there. When someone dies the whole village comes to the funeral. We all walk up the hill, silent, taking it in turn to carry the coffin, listening to the church bell below, grateful for the presence of family and neighbours.

Try to go there some time. You will be out of breath when you arrive. Look around at the sarcophagi, note the names: Papavassilis, Orfanos, Protopapas. These are the names that are still in our village today. Look at the ages; eighty-one, ninety-three, eighty-seven. In the old times, once you got past your early years you could live a long, long time. The wind blows here; now a low, soft moan, now a gale to buff your ears and belt your body. Then you have to lean into the wind to move forward and take care when you turn the corner by the church. You can hear the creak of the old windmill too, but be careful if you come here in the evening, make certain that you do not frighten yourself, for you will not be alone. In the corner, by the wall, most days there will be a figure, an old lady, dark clothes from head to foot, her shawl pulled over her face. She sits there silent and still, looking out to sea, saying nothing, searching the distance.

Her story is a sad one. She comes from the village, but lived away in Kos for some time. She was born here before the war, but had to leave when the war came. It is complicated, but I will try to explain. Karin, for that is her name, lived with her mother and her father. She was their only child and they loved her. Early life here was happy; she went to school in the mornings and helped her mother, or played with the children on the beach, in the afternoon. Sometimes she helped her father clean the nets and loved to see the numbers of fish and the different kinds of fish that he caught. Her life continued in this easy way and as she grew it was clear, from the way the young men looked at her, that she would be a beautiful woman. Even the war did not impinge on this happiness at first. There were good rains in the winters of '41 and '42, so the summer harvests were good; there was wheat and barley, oil and honey. The British had been defeated, but the Germans had not yet come and the Italians continued in their lazy, benevolent way.

Then Karin fell in love with a young fisher boy, slim, blond, smart. An orphan named Dimitris, he lived with his aunt in a little stone house by the sea and he fished all hours that he could. His boat was the smallest in the village, a wooden, white painted boat, with a dark red sail and he was out all hours and in all seas. His aunt had no land, they had no money and he could not afford long nets, so he had to fish for many hours to feed the two of them and to catch enough fish to barter for oil and flour. Dimitris had left school at the age of twelve, but he could read and write, but he was a sensitive young boy and he too fell in love. It happened slowly at first. He helped her father, sometimes, in rough seas, pulling in the heavy nets while her father worked the oars. This is difficult work and dangerous too. Dimitris would stand on the wet, slippery prow, reach down, pull the nets up and into the boat. Her father would row slowly forward, keeping the boat at an angle to the nets to ease the strain on the net and to make it easier for the boy. This is skilful work even in a dead calm sea, but when the Meltemi blows, it is very hard and Dimitris would need all his strong physique to balance on the wet deck, his bare feet taking what purchase they could as the boat plunged and rose through two metre waves. Difficult and dangerous and exhausting too, but there were fish and fish is food and food is life. The rule in the village is a share for the boat owner, a share for the net and a share for each fisherman. This would mean only one quarter for Dimitris, but Karin's father was a kind man and he liked the young boy, so everything was split evenly. Down the line, we say. Sometimes too, in the winter, Dimitris was invited home to eat *kakaviar*, a special soup made from three kinds of fish. He would be given a place by the fire and sit there in the smoke, with wooden spoon and clay bowl eating the thick soup and rough, brown bread. He would look up sometimes and see Karin's face searching his own, her eyes gleaming through the smoke, in that dark, candlelit, rough, simple room.

So began the story of Karin and Dimitris. A glance here, a touch there and soon they would find their paths crossed; by accident at first and then they fell into meeting regularly. Dimitris would offer to help milk the goats and Karin would find herself freeing the fish from his nets. Love is a wonderful thing for young people and their lives were happy as the wind blew and the seasons changed and flowers bloomed and faded. They were together often now and walked through the woods and lay down in the shelter of *kaliopus*, the wind-bent, ancient, pine trees. They tried to keep the customs of the village, but they were young, the war was coming closer and they did not know how long this life would last, so they did what was natural and they were happy as they lay together. The birds of passage, the passerines and eagles, the hawks and the Eleanora falcons, came and went two times and then the Germans came and everything changed. The Italians knew they were defeated; they did not want to fight anymore. The Germans took some of them away while others hid in caves in the mountains. The atmosphere had changed, there was menace about, there was fear in the houses, in the harbour, in the hills. There was less food now; the rain did not come and the harvest was not good. There could be no trade with the islands under British control and they had to feed the Germans. And then one of the German officers began to notice Karin and her parents knew she had to go away.

There was one boat with an engine in the village then; a fishing boat with a sail too, small, but safe. Slowly over a period of weeks the parents went from family to family, begging, buying and borrowing provisions. Germans were bribed, diesel oil changed hands, something was going to happen. Neither Karin, nor Dimitris, nor anyone knew that she was pregnant, not formally that is, but Karin glowed with life and colour and Dimitris clucked around her and loved her so and they knew in some unspoken, secret way that they were now three. They were going to be a family. Karin did not want to leave, but she knew she had to, or something bad would happen between Dimitris and the officer, and anyway, Dimitris would follow. So one night Karin, her mother and father and four other villagers slid away in the fishing boat. Oars first, muffled with old clothes, then the sail and out to sea the engine took them into the black night to Kos, British control and safety.

The Germans were angry about what had happened; they strutted and shouted round the village, they cuffed Dimitris, but did not beat him badly. They too were losing the war, a long way from home, in a hard, hard place. They were frightened, unpredictable and dangerous. Dimitris was sad, but not devastated; he kept quiet, he had hope, his turn would come. The winds here always follow the same pattern; in the summer there is the Meltemi from the north, then in September or early October that wind dies and the Sirocco comes from the south. Dimitris would wait for that change and sail his little boat north to Kos, Karin and safety. He would sail at night, lie up, or row in the day and it would take him three days. He told nobody of his plans.

Over the summer he worked hard; drying and salting fish, drying octopus and exchanging fresh fish for olive oil, cheese and flour, so his aunt would not be left without food when he went away. Then he waited. The weather was strange that year and the Sirocco did not arrive until late, but Dimitris was patient. He waited and he waited, till one day there was a strong wind from the south and he knew the time had come. There was a curfew in the village at that time; boats could only leave the village with permission and none after dark. The curfew was enforced by four German soldiers, old men, veterans from the Russian front. They took it in eight-hour turns, two on, two off, all day, every day, patrolling the village, the beach and the harbour. It was boring work and tiring and often, after dark, disobeying orders, the four of them would be seen together, gossiping and drinking raki in the little *cafeneion*. They were there on the night that Dimitris sailed away. Taking with him food and water for a week, Dimitris untied his boat from the mole and leaving his anchor in the water, so as not to make a noise with the chain, he allowed the current to take him away. The *cafeneion* had an oil lamp and

Dimitris could see the silhouettes of the soldiers as he drifted away, their grey helmets resting on the wall outside. Soon he rowed, keeping close to the island and then, hoisting his sail he was off, the water singing under his little boat, on his way to Karin, to his baby, to love and the future. He was not frightened, he was young, he was happy. Life was good.

By the morning he was close to Halki. When the light came he lowered his sail, so as not to be seen, and rowed close to the uninhabited and rocky west coast. Sheltered from the Sirocco, he found a tiny stretch of calm sea, between rocks under a great, grey cliff. There he tied his boat. He slept, ate a little dried bread and salty goats cheese, picked limpets and cockles from the rocks for protein and set off again as the red, autumn sun fell into the soft, white clouds to the west. Now it was open sea and more difficult. He had not been this far before, but he knew that Kos was directly to the north and a big island and he knew the pole star. So he did not worry as he sped through the night, four knots or five, he wasn't sure, but the wind was *prima, prima*, directly astern and that's the easiest to sail in and to do this work in the dark. Morning came and he was alone in the sea. That was Rhodes over there to the east and to the north that long, low, smudge of clouds signified Kos and maybe Turkey. The sea was oily now, with a swell; the wind had dropped a little, but still came from the right quarter. He was in a kind of no mans land, but at sea. The British controlled the skies and what few German patrol boats there were feared to come this far in the daytime, so Dimitris kept his little, red sail high. He was going to be with Karin, to kiss her neck, to bite, to smell the sun in her dark curls. He did not worry, he was young and God was good. Then, a sudden act of random violence.

The boy flying the Spitfire was the same age as Dimitris. Let's call him Roger and let's say he was on his first patrol in his brand new plane. He had never fired his four 30 mm cannon in anger, never felt the excitement or fear of hunting, or of being hunted, but his pulse beat fast and he sang to himself at the thrill of being alone in the sky, knowing that over there on the south of that big island, were Messerschmitts and Heinkels. Maybe on the ground and maybe, even now, being prepared for take off and battle. The war was coming to an end and Roger wanted to make his mark, to stand with the older pilots, to be known as an ace. His orders were to fly low, patrol a box to the north and west of Rhodes and to report any shipping movements. Roger liked to fly low, very low. He was less then twenty metres up, covering the water at a hundred metres every second. He steadied to clear his guns, to fire a burst of two seconds. He pulled the nose of the plane up a little, levelled out, pressed the button and at that exact moment saw a little red sail. Dimitris saw nothing, heard nothing, knew nothing He had lashed an oar to the stern and leant on it to steer. Half asleep, half awake he looked north, always north, a smile, a dream, an adventure and then he was not there. One cannon shell, hitting the water at an oblique angle, burst into twenty or more fragments, one destroyed Dimitris, others hit the boat and punctured the sail. Roger saw none of this, he looked in the mirror, saw the boat sailing on.

Thank Christ, he thought, thank Christ, I could have hit the bloody thing.

Dimitris was gone, but the boat sailed on for a while and in Kos, above a village on a hillside near the church, Karin sat and waited. Every day she went there as the sun went down. She knew she was pregnant now, she ran her hands along the outline of the bump. Soon he would come. Soon he would come. Was that a red sail, or the sun, or the sun's rays on something floating in the water? Was that the crest of a wave or foam or a white boat? So difficult to see, so easy to dream in the warmth of the evening, knowing that you are loved and in the safety of Kos.

Having a baby without a father was not easy in those days. Having a blonde baby was manna to the gossips. But when Karin and her family returned to our village after the war our people knew who the father was. They did not know what had happened to Dimitris. They knew when he left; they thought they knew why. They did not know why he did not come back. Perhaps one day he would return. These things happen.

Time passed. Difficult times passed. Karin buried her pain, did her duty, looked after her parents and brought up her adored son. She loved him, she cared for him. Her miniature Dimitris brought so much happiness. Time passed and her parents died and she was left alone with her son. He grew older, older than Dimitris had been, but he did not find a love of his own. He stayed with his mother, knowing of her loss, knowing she could not bear another. So she was content for a while, but old age plays tricks on old people; memories return, more intense, more real than reality. That's why, nearly eighty years old now, Karin sits there, looking out to sea, looking for a familiar red sail. We will join her, wait by the church to catch our breath, make a noise so as not to startle her.

Den erthei mekri tora, she says. He did not come yet.

Oki , mekri tora den erthei. Issos avrio. Ella, manna mou, pame. Enai krio edw. No he didn't come yet. Maybe tomorrow. Mother, come home. It's cold here and the wind is strong. Come home and sit by the fire while I make soup. Come, before it gets dark.

How to Fish

Tourists who come to the village think of it as a fishing village, that all of us are fishermen and that we all use nets. They are wrong on all counts. Only a handful of villagers fish for a living, the rest potter around with varying degrees of enthusiasm and success. Some of them with no success at all. There are many ways to fish with and without nets. The technique used will depend on the season, the weather, the boat and the fish being hunted. It will also depend on how hungry you are.

Let us take nets for example. Fishermen from Kalymnos and further afield come here in big boats, 15 metres or more, and trawl, indiscriminately hoovering up fish and fauna and destroying the coral and the sea bed prairies that are precious feeding grounds for many species. These fishermen lead a hard life. They sleep on blankets on their nets, turn by turn, two on, two off, working day and night. There are no toilets on their boats, no fresh water for washing. There are no showers. Sometimes they come to the village for an hour or two to wait for the ferry boat, so they can ship their catch to Rhodes. They come to Anna's to buy chocolate and lemonade and then queue up, ragged and barefoot, to phone mothers, wives and girlfriends to say that they are all right and to ask for news. If you look closely at the crew on these boats you will notice that they resemble one another. They are father and sons, or a group of brothers, or an uncle with nephews. Sometimes it is a couple with their children leading this nomadic life. What they all have in common is a desire to make money and retire. I once asked a friend of mine if he liked the life of a fisherman. He thought for a while:

What I want is a small house with a balcony by the sea. I want to sit there and eat *souvlaki* every day.

As well as trawling, the big boats also lay out drift nets to catch fish as they go to feed off the beaches in the evening and as they return to deep water in the morning. Locals also use drift nets, but as our boats are smaller the nets are not so long and we can discriminate as to the species we catch. Sometimes we use much smaller nets to catch small fish called *atherinos*. The system is to cast the net in a loop along the rocky coast, throw stones to drive the little fish into the net and then pull the net into the boat carefully so that the fish are scooped up. While one man can do this alone the process can be time consuming. It may take several attempts to find a shoal of fish and if you catch them it takes a long time to extract them from the nets. Still, they are tasty and good bait and, if you have company and it is not too windy, this is a pleasant way to fish.

Atherinos are used as bait for *katheti*, a lightweight line used vertically with a weight and four hooks. *Katheti* are mainly used to catch *perka* and *hannos* which are the ingredients of a good fish soup. Only in Greece does it make sense to go fishing for soup. *Atherinos* are also used as bait for *paragadi*. Most visitors will have seen baskets around the village full of nylon line and with hundreds of hooks along the rim. That is a *paragadi*. The line can be up to one kilometre long and, every three metres, side lines with a hook are tied at right angles. The nylon is heavyweight and expensive and so are the hooks. It can take two to three days to make a *paragadi*, hours to catch the bait and several hours to hook the bait to the *paragadi*. Then you go and throw it into the sea! But you do not throw it anywhere. You decide the type of fish you want to catch and you lay the line over rocks at the depth and at the time where those fish will be feeding. Often you lay the line out at dusk and pick it up two or more hours later in the dark. I won't tell you the best spots to fish with *paragadi*. That is my secret. But I will tell you that if you are rowing a boat, or using your engine to go slowly as the line is laid out in the dark and large baited hooks are whizzing by your ear, then you had better trust your partner.

There are many forms of fishing that have evolved over the years. Perhaps the most esoteric and maybe the most ancient is sexual fishing for *sepia*. These are harmless little creatures from the same family as octopus and squid. Under the water, in the daylight, if you see them as you dive, they are transparent as glass and stunningly beautiful. They are also tasty. The system is to catch a female *sepia* as she comes into the rocks to lay her eggs. You do this with a small net on the end of a pole. You make certain that it is indeed a female, not an easy task, tie her to the boat with a hook and line and row slowly along the shore. Suddenly she changes colour, black and white stripes run electrically up and down her body. A male is ready to pounce! When it does, you scoop up the surprised suitor with your net and put it into a bucket of water. You have to hurry, however, or you will be sprayed with black ink.

Generally, the smaller the boat the smarter the fisherman has to be, the more selective they can be and the less damage they do to the environment. Hand line fishing is generally more ecological than fishing with nets, but the most ecological method is diving or spear fishing. When you dive, you see the fish, you know how big it is and you decide whether or not to kill it. You can decide only to kill mature fish that have bred and thus ensure there are fish for future generations. Diving can be exciting and dangerous. It is also a psychedelic experience. Nothing prepares you for the sunburst of colours, nor the light and life all around you as you enter this strange and alien world. It is addictive as you dive down, again and again. You try to relax to save energy. You don't swim down, but glide, letting gravity and the weights round your waist do the work. I only dive to around ten metres, but the air seems far away when you are that deep and you are on the edge of panic as you swim up to the silver surface. Your breath is gone, and your strength, and there is no margin for error. Hour after hour you dream of big fish. You see a shadow under a rock or at the entrance to a cave; you dive, you hover. Nothing. Back to the surface. You see the shadow again, a tail perhaps. A bit deep for you, but possible. Position yourself, take two deep breaths, hold your nose to protect your eardrums and glide down, arm and harpoon gun out at full stretch. It is a fish. Slowly come close, slowly, slowly. The fish sees you, you fire. Hit. An explosion of blood and scales and you swim gently to the surface, making sure not to lose the fish from the harpoon. It is a nice one, a sea bream . Supper. Agony as it fights, as you carefully transfer it from the harpoon to your line and move on to look for the next fish and the next and the next. Hours pass. This is hypnotic work, addictive, but tiring. The sea is calm now, the sun going down. You swim to the boat and put your gun inside. You unbuckle the weights carefully, so as not to lose them, and heave them over the side. Now the difficult part. You grab the side of the boat, push yourself under the sea, then up like a cork and over, flippers flailing, chest heaving and you are in the boat. The entry lacks dignity, but brings a sense of relief. Anchored off shore alone, if you can't get into the boat you are dead.

There are more than twenty ways of fishing here, but whatever the method there is one certainty. There are less fish now than there were, even ten years ago. If the slaughter and the pollution and destruction of habitat continues there will be no fish left. Your children will not know of the magic of the sea, or the taste of fresh fish. Some of us try to fish in a sustainable way. The customers could insist that we all fish sensibly. All you have to do is ask.

Michaelis and the Crane

Most fishermen from Kalymnos and other islands work in family groups, two, three, or four at a time. They leave home early in the year and return in November with calloused hands and feet and, if they are lucky, with money in their pockets. The traditional division of money is one share for the owner of the boat, one for the owner of the nets and one for each crew member. Thus, if the captain owns the boat and the nets and works with two other men, he gets three sixths of the profit and they get one sixth each. You can see that, under this system, everybody wants to own their own nets and their own boat. Some men travel with their wives, or even wives and children; school is skipped, work is shared and you can see mothers and five and six year-old children doing their bit. The fishermen live in the extremely cramped and primitive quarters of a nine or ten metre boat, without toilets, showers, running water, fridge or cooker and sometimes without beds.

Some men work alone in a boat, but normally they fish close to home or team up with another boat. They do this for company and for safety. The one exception that I know of is Michaelis. It is difficult to describe Michaelis without making him out to be a joke or turning him into a caricature. I only know his first name and I do not know him well. We have met a few times and each time there is a party and everybody eats fish. He is a little man, short and slight in build. Michaelis has a large boat, over fifteen metres, and he travels alone. He stays at sea, far out at sea, three or four weeks on end. He is different from all other fishermen that we know. When he comes to the village he sits in one or other bar, bare feet tucked under himself, gossiping and drinking. Hunched up, his wizened face brown from the wind and from the sun, he looks just like a little pet monkey. Michaelis eats fish and only fish; fish soup for breakfast, fish stew for lunch and grilled fish when he is on land. He smells like a fish; his skin, his clothes, his sweat smell of fish and also of salt. We sit around him listening to his news and laughing at his stories and we form a *parea*, or group, and we have fun. Michaelis does not accept that beer is alcohol, referring to it as a fizzy drink. Only whisky or ouzo is alcohol. Sometimes he drinks these too and when he gets drunk he sings. He does not sing our songs, our *mantinades*. No, he sings songs from the other islands; from Kos, Kalymnos, Kassos, from Halki, Rhodos and Crete. When he is sad he drinks whisky and he sings bitter songs, of blood and betrayal and the loneliness of a man alone in the ocean. When he is happy and the ice box on his boat is full of fish, he drinks ouzo. We all do and then his voice is soft and sweet and we hear melodies and songs describing flowers on the hills in the springtime and the rhythm in the steps of young girls as they hold hands and dance pretty circles round a village square.

Michaelis fishes all day and every day, at every depth in every way possible. He describes these to us and we sit until the early hours and discuss the merits of different fish and the ways of catching them. We talk about knots and lines and nets and the old sea salts washed up on the shores of the Aegean and we move from the fizzy drink to the harder stuff. Michaelis knows much about the sea. He has caught strange fish that no one has seen before and can't be found in books. He has seen whales and dolphins, turtles, giant manta rays and great white sharks. Travelling for so long and for so far, Michaelis finds many things in the sea; sometimes useful things, sometimes sad. He once found a boat, by itself, far out at sea, bobbing in the waves, its oars tucked carefully away, the engine in good condition, the tank full of fuel. Perfect, but empty. A good boat is worth money and if you find something at sea, it belongs to you by law. Michaelis took it in tow, went to the nearest island, registered his find with the police, sold the boat and had a party.

There are other things he has found too, things which aren't so good. A body for example, a body upside down, hands, hair and legs spread out like a swimmer eternally snorkelling above a ghostly reef. What do you do when you find a body at sea? You use a boat hook or a sling you bring it aboard, taking care not to look at the face. If you have a strong stomach, or are very greedy, you check the pockets. You open a hatch and move some fish around the ice box. You slide the body in, you radio the port police and get to the nearest port as fast as possible. But the strangest thing that he has found is a crane, a floating crane, the kind used to build harbours and ports. He hasn't told us the story himself, but the story has travelled the islands without him.

What we heard is that the weather was bad, the sea was rough, force eight Beaufort, and Michaelis was a long way from home, a very long way from any home. At force eight the sea whips the spray from the tops of waves, blinding you as it comes horizontal into your face or covers the window of your cabin as you curse the mother that bore you and threaten to do something very rude to Eve, the mother of mankind, with a piece of the holy cross. The storm lasted two days and Michaelis, being alone, had to stay at the wheel all that time. It was dusk on the second day and in the lowering light, Michaelis peered through the spray and saw something huge and black above the waves. He was barely awake, totally exhausted and close to hallucinating. He thought he had come across some long lost harbour, he thought he had died and found a port in a storm, he thought he had lost his mind. But he shone his powerful light and saw, waving at him, twenty metres high, a floating crane. He also saw a fortune. These things are worth a lot of money. If he could get a line to it, if he could take it in tow, if he could get it home, if, if, if. . . He tried to think clearly. Two weeks at sea speaking only to himself, two days without sleep and now this. The crane's platform, black in the dark, was pitching and heaving, too dangerous to go alongside with the boat, but he had to get a line to it. There was only one way. He would have to swim. He took his boat downwind, found a light rope, tied one end to a heavy rope and the other round his waist, put his engine in neutral, took off his clothes and dived into the sea. Just like that. No hesitation, no thought, and he is in huge waves in a force eight gale far from the nearest land. Fifty metres on he grabs the ladder on the side of the platform. This wrenches him three metres into the air and plunges him back down under the sea. His arms ache, his knees and elbows bleed from the barnacles, but he keeps hold of the ladder as it pitches wildly in the dark and slowly, carefully, climbs out of the sea. He is on deck now, looking for the right bollard in the right place. There. He pulls on the light line, pulls the strong rope across the seething void and ties the crane to his boat. Then, this tiny, naked man stands on the edge of the platform, waits for a high wave to come close and the platform to tilt and dives into the sea again. It is easier now. Using the rope to pull himself across the black, boiling gap he gets back aboard his boat, gets to the cabin and collapses. He has swum 100 metres in that sea and he has tied himself to a fortune. He stands up, steaming in the dark in a pool of salt water and salt blood, grabs a bottle and starts to drink whisky by the neck, a happy little monkey, Michaelis dries himself, dresses, warms up some soup and eats. Later, he lengthens the line to his crane, then folds himself into his bunk and falls asleep, dreaming of bounty, of reward, of money.

Four hours later and dawn is near; the sky is light in the east and the wind is not so strong. Michaelis revs the engine and slowly, very slowly, he sets off for home. As the light comes he can see the name of the company painted on the side of the crane. He uses his VHF, contacts the port police, tells them of his find and waits. Two hours later and there is an incoming call from the company.

    I have your crane.
    What crane?
    Your crane.
    Don't be stupid.
    I have your crane.
    I will call back.

Two hours pass.

    You have our crane.
    Yes.
    Where?

He tells them.

    Is it damaged?
    Seems OK.
    What do you want?
    A million.
    Drachmas?
    Dollars.
    Malakas. A million dollars? You are stupid.
    Call me back.

He closes down the VHF.

Three hours pass. The VHF again.

    Yes?

How about a hundred thousand?
Dollars?
Yes.
Let's talk.

So, throughout the day they talk. They don't agree the price, Michaelis now wants five hundred thousand dollars, but as they talk Michaelis gets closer to the port, closer to home, closer to real money. Hour after hour steering with care, so as not to break the rope, travelling at two or three knots, he gets closer to port. But his mind is elsewhere; he is spending money, travelling to strange places, staying in hotels, hotels with sheets and towels and a fridge in the room and really big beds. A house for his mother, with a balcony, a new boat, a pleasure boat and lazy, lazy days. No more fishing, no more loneliness, no more . . . no more. He has to concentrate; the crane is not easy to tow. It is forty tons in weight and twenty metres high, so that even a light wind takes it, and it slowly snakes from side to side and tilts one way and then the other. But his island is on the horizon now and tomorrow, at dawn, he will be home and rich.

Michaelis is on the VHF two or three times during the day, but the owners will not budge. Michaelis is smart, he believes that the closer to port, the more the crane is worth. The time of the hard working fisherman has come. At night he stops, puts lights on all over his boat to warn any passing ships of a hazard and lies down in his cabin. Of course he cannot sleep, his mind is full of images — of wealth, parties, silk, clothes, shoes, sheets, oh sheets and pillows, and the smell of expensive perfume.

He is up at dawn in the morning, heads to the port, hoves to outside the port and gets on the VHF.

I am here.
Good.
Where do you want me to take the crane?

Lets agree the price first.
What's the offer?
I offer you five.
Five hundred thousand?

Michaelis heart pumps like a new four stroke outboard motor.

Don't be stupid. Five thousand.

Michaelis cannot hear.

Say that again.
Five thousand.

He is ice cold, the four stroke has stopped, but the brain is racing.

There must be some mistake. You offered me one hundred thousand.
Sure, but you didn't accept.
Five?
Five
Fuck you *malakas*.
I am not *malakas*. You are *malakas*.
For five you don't get the crane.
So keep it.
What? Keep it? What the fuck am I going to do with a crane? Where will I anchor it? Suppose there's a storm. It's dangerous.
Friend that is not my problem. You are the legal owner of the crane. If it sinks you are the owner of the wreck. If a ferry boat hits the wreck, you pay. You can't pay, you go to jail. Five thousand dollars is a generous offer in these circumstances.
Fuck you.
Good morning to you captain. Thank you for fetching the crane.
Fuck you.

He switches off the VHF, goes out on deck, kicks some nets, kicks ropes, kicks a big red float, punches the side of his cabin, bangs his head against the window, sits down, stand up, curses. The curse is long and loud and this time includes doing something spectacular to the whore Eve with a piece of the one true cross, while the homosexual Adam suffers a greater indignity, and on and on. After two minutes of deep profanity Michaelis stretches his arms out, looks up at the sky and screams *Yiati* (why)?*Yiati? Yiati?*

We don't know much else. We hear he talked to the port police, but they would not let him bring the crane into the harbour. We hear he set off for another destination and later was seen outside Kos. What happened next we do not know, but he's out there somewhere, wandering the ocean, an ancient mariner with a very large albatross. We wait for him and one day he will come again. Perhaps in a yacht, or in his fishing boat. Maybe, one day, we will see something strange and dark on the horizon, waving like a giant arm far out to sea. After a day or more we might see that it is Michaelis with his crane. We have only a small harbour here so we will have to go out to him in our little boats. We will take him some beer for refreshments, but I am not sure if whisky or ouzo would be more appropriate. We will see.

The Junta

Many of us are fortunate enough to live in countries where, in the main, a fair and benign rule of law is in place and a knock on the door is not considered a sinister event. Consequently very few of us have had to make a stand against totalitarianism or dictatorship. We are untested. This is not true of Greece. Following the Second World War, came the Civil War and later the rule of the Colonels or the Junta. Greek people had to struggle against dictatorship well into the nineteen eighties and it was not until Greece joined the EU that democracy properly returned to its birthplace. Greeks well know the difficulties of living under dictators.

The village was not immune from these struggles. After the war, many of our people were not allowed to return to the place of their birth and even when they were allowed back into the country they could not claim the pensions and entitlements that were their due. The sole reason for this discrimination being that during the struggle against the German occupiers they had fought with the only serious resistance army on the mainland, ELAS. Later, in the time of the Colonels, the village was used as a place of exile. Dissidents were punished by being sent to this isolated place, far from Athens. We were a gulag.

Living under a dictatorship leads to turmoil, conflict and betrayal. Choices and decisions have to be made on a daily basis; honesty and decency are constantly tested. One such choice was made during the time of the Colonels by someone from the village, let us call him Nikos. I have known this man for over twenty years, but only recently heard his story.

Nikos was in the navy at the time, in the 1970's, a conscript, an ordinary seaman, smart, hardworking, determined to keep his head down, and paid 40 drachmas a week. Then, his captain, without consulting with the crew, declared opposition to the Junta and sailed off to Italy to seek political asylum. The captain was left there and Nikos and the rest of the crew were fetched back in disgrace to Piraeus. Under deep suspicion they were confined to shore duties only. As part of his duties Nikos found himself working aboard a prison ship. By prisoners we mean left-wing opponents to the Colonels, some anonymous, some named, some famous. These prisoners were kept in lockers in the scuppers of an old barge in the harbour. A new prisoner arrived and Nikos was told to take a cup of tea down to him. Without a word the prisoner knocked it out of his hand. Nikos did not understand.

Why do you do this?

I am on hunger strike.

The officers asked what had happened. He told them. They sent men down to beat up the prisoner. They sent Nikos down with another cup of tea.

Please drink this or they will beat you again.

I will not drink it. But tell them I did.

And he poured away the tea.

So Nikos lied to the officers and the hunger strike continued until the prisoner was found unconscious and taken to hospital. The ensuing publicity led to concessions being made. The prisoner commenced to eat and was returned to the barge. By now Nikos and the prisoner shared a few words every day. Until, pressing a shred of paper with a scribbled address down Nikos shirt, the prisoner asked

Go to my wife. Tell her I am alive.

A moment of truth. A time to decide. If you do not, can you face the prisoner again? Or yourself? If you do and you are caught, what will happen? Who will care for your family? Will they know? Will you end up here? Whose side are you on?

Nikos asked himself these questions as he walked around Piraeus that night. He walked for hours seeking answers, at the same time making certain he was not followed. Then, suddenly, he was at the address and knocking gently on the door.

Nothing.

He knocked louder.

Nothing.

Louder again.

Who is it?

What to say? Only, I am Nikos.

Nikos who?

Nikos, from your husband.

The door opens a little. An eye sees his uniform, notices he is only an ordinary seaman and not an officer. The door opens further, a face looking around for others an arm drags him inside. The door closes.

My husband? Alive? Oh God, Oh God, Oh God.

And Nikos is drowned in tears and kisses and relief and gratitude.

He only went there the once, but that was enough. Husband and wife were in contact. Each knew that the other was all right. Each had renewed strength to continue the struggle.

We are led to believe that struggles against oppression are won by superhuman acts of heroic individuals. Sometimes this might be the case. More often it is the small acts of resistance by a myriad of heroes that topple despots and dictators. Heroes who want to look at themselves every day in the mirror and don't think to mention what they have done. Not until they are drunk and thirty years have gone by.

The Mermaid and the Hunchback

Because of our rich cultural traditions, many folklorists and anthropologists come to the village. They record our music, photograph the women and interview the old people. Often they send us learned papers from this or that university and we are grateful for their attempts to explain to us what we are. Normally what they write is correct, but because they are anthropologists or ethnomusicologists or some other ologist they turn our living culture into something dry and segmented. They miss the big picture, which is that our life and traditions, our music, work, food, clothes and landscape, are entwined and connected and that our culture is still evolving. Too often we are left with the impression that something has been taken away from us and we have nothing in return. One exception is a man who came here two years ago. He came to search for a legend and left us with a story.

I met him one evening at the Gorgona, an Italian restaurant run by my good friends Gigi and Gabriella. The food is good there, but sometimes the service is not, so I always go to the kitchen to place my order and to tell Gabri where I will be sitting. This is a wise precaution because, down from the terrace, on the little plaza by the fountain, it is dark and you could sit there for hours without being noticed. Indeed Gabriella told me there was someone sitting there waiting to meet me. Back down the steps I went and found him sitting in the darkest corner, by the vine. He had a kind face, but did not stand as we shook hands and I had the feeling that he had some kind of physical problem. Drinks arrived and we started to talk. He told me he was a professor and that he was from Athens, but his accent and some dialect words told me he had some island connection. His interest was in collecting stories about mermaids. He wanted to know if we had such stories and were there any old people who claimed to have seen them and, if so, where were they sighted. I know many things about the village, but people here do not talk about mermaids. We have seals and several kinds of dolphins and some people cast spells and carry charms to ward off the evil eye at sea, but there are no direct stories of mermaids. The nearest is that some fishermen have heard voices in the dark, as if the sea is calling to them, and when the sea is wild and dangerous they have an urge to go over the side and gently surrender to the waves.

There was a note of sadness about this man, but he seemed open and friendly and he had a gentle voice. As the evening wore on and we drank more and more, his story began to unfold.

It started with a young man called Pablos, a hunchback, a big man with powerful arms and deeply tanned face. Pablos lived with his mother in a small house near the beach, on an island not far from here. He was a fisherman, a good fisherman, setting out his nets every night as the sun set over the mountain and pulling them in each morning as the sun rose from the sea. He kept his nets in a cave by the sea and every morning he would sit there in the shade, his strong nimble fingers cleaning his nets and sorting the fish. The catch was never great, but enough to feed himself and his mother, with a little left over to sell and even some to give to the beach children. These were the children of the poor and the prostitute's bastard children, an unruly mass of noisy, snotty, ragamuffins, who spent all day, every day, on the beach. They were his friends.

Each morning he would snooze a little in the cave, then walk up the beach to his mother's house. She would take the fish and make him coffee while he sat outside in the shade. Later the women of the village would come and buy fish and he would sit and listen happily to them gossiping together. His mother was an old lady now, but she still worked hard, collecting food for the goats, feeding the chickens, salting fish and cleaning their little house. He had lived like this for a long time, fishing, working, sleeping in the sun. Days, months, years drifting past. He asked for little else. Bar girls came to his cave from time to time and the occasional bohemian tourist, but no one had moved him. The life of a hunchback is not easy and, until he was big enough to fight with fist and boot, his childhood had been hard. He did not share his deeper thoughts easily. He was defensive, but an amusing and interesting man and the people from the village sought his company. And then the earth tilted on its axis and everything changed.

It was a strange relationship, a sophisticated foreigner from the city and a poor fisherman. They met one night, a warm night with a calm sea, a yoghurt sea, pale silver from the low, full moon. She was sitting on a rock with bare feet plashing in the waves and eddies. He saw her as he walked along the beach towards his cave. He saw she was alone and he spoke gently to her and kept his distance so that she would not be frightened in the dark. They talked a long time about their lives and about themselves and their dreams.

She told him about the city, her white painted flat, the church nearby and the bells that rang the hour and the siren of the ferry boat as it arrived at five o'clock each day. She told him about the husband who had left her, without money, to bring up their daughter alone. She talked about living alone now and teaching and the children in the school and cycling to work in the early morning traffic.

He talked to her about the sea, about fish and fishing and the dangers of fishing alone with lead-weighted nets that could catch your feet and drag you down. He told her about the hooks caught in his hands and the barbs from the fish and the burns from the nylon line. He told her about the villagers too, about his old mother living in the small house on the beach and about the father who had disappeared after he was born.

They talked for hours in the darkness, serious sometimes, but with laughter too, for he had a fast tongue and she liked his humour. Then they grew tired and after a long silence, he gently asked her and she said yes, she would like to come with him in his boat to pick up the nets in the morning. They said goodnight and she walked away, barefoot and slim, balanced, quiet and thoughtful. Nothing had been said about his back and all night he was restless, fretting and turning and dreaming, with her voice in his ears and her walk in his mind's eye.

In the morning he saw her lit by the blood red sun as it rose from the end of the sea. He was in the open now. He could not hide his back. He was tense and unsure until they were out to sea and collecting the nets. She was strong and could pull the nets into the boat as he rowed. When the nets were stuck and it needed skill as well as strength to free them from the rocks and he needed to stand on the front of the boat to do this work, then she helped with the oars. They were pleased to be working together. As they worked, when they touched, they felt a little awkward, but the touch felt good.

It was a good catch. They went to a beach and, while he cleaned the nets and laid the fish carefully in boxes, she walked some way from the boat, took off her clothes and swam. He didn't look, but when she came to the boat again he could see that she was still wet as her dress stuck to her body. Now he did look and he could see that he really liked her, but he said nothing. And she looked into his face and she liked the honesty of it and his colour and the little scars above his eyes. She looked at his back, but she said nothing. They returned to the village, anchored the boat and carried the nets to the cave.

Our hunchback has caught a mermaid, said the gossips and early risers, as the happy couple flaunted themselves in the sun while taking the fish to his house. She met his mother. His mother asked her name.

My name is Ioanna, but my friends call me Annie

Come to supper Annie and I will cook soup.

Ioanna said she would, but first cycled to the town to rest and to change and to think about what was happening to her. In the evening she returned with a bottle of wine and they sat side by side on a rough bench in the smokiness of his mother's house. They ate *kakaviar*, a thick fish soup, and strong, crusty bread. His mother watched over them without speaking. The wine was good wine and when they had finished the bottle he waited a while and then he poured a glass each of rough, local brandy and the two of them sat outside in the shadow of the house and talked softly in the cool breeze. Then she had to go and he walked with her to her bike. He wanted to touch her, to put his arm around her, but he was nervous. He wanted to kiss her, but they did not kiss.

She returned the next weekend. He took her to a beach away from the village and this time he did look when she took off her clothes, but tenderly, for despite his size and his strength he was a shy man. He kept his shirt on as he collected handfuls of thin, dark, seaweed and shellfish from the rocks. Then he dived and caught an octopus and he made a present for her of sun-dried salt that he gathered

The Mermaid and the Hunchback

from high rocks. When they returned to the village it was evening and he fetched draught red wine from the taverna and bread from his house, while she gathered driftwood. She lit a fire at the entrance to the cave, as he beat the octopus on nearby rocks to make it soft and washed it twice in the sea to give it taste. They drank wine and ate shellfish and barbecued the octopus and ate it with bread and raw seaweed, tasting of sex and iodine. Sometimes they touched and once he kissed her on the forehead and then they touched more and so he bent down and ran his lips along her neck and felt her shiver and squeeze herself inside. Then their arms were around one another and they kissed and kissed and kissed again. They stood trembling by the fire. He wanted her to be sure, so he tried to wait, but their skin was alive and they had to touch one another. So he took her hand and they went into the cave. Without words they found themselves wrapped in blankets on the floor of the cave with their clothes strewn around them. They made love and it was good between them. She reached her hand and touched him on his back where the bones were deformed. Only his mother had touched him there, and as she stroked his back, he cried soft tears of relief and joy and she loved him and he loved her.

By now the voice of the professor was too soft. He said something I could not hear and I asked him to repeat it.

They slept like spoons, he told me, like spoons in a drawer.

In the morning, when they awoke, they made love again and everything was easy. They lay in each others arms and he looked deep into her eyes and they could smell one another on their bodies and taste salt and sex on their skins and they lay on the earth and the earth felt good.

Each week was the same. She would come to him on the Saturday afternoon and leave late on the Sunday. They would go in his boat along the rocky coast to fish and to swim. They would return to the cave or go to the house to sit with his mother and they would play with the beach children. In the evening Ioanna would read to him from newspapers, for he loved to hear about big cities and foreign places and he loved to hear her city voice and to see her wearing glasses. Occasionally they would go to the taverna and sit there, shy and embarrassed to be in company, and the village people would be happy to see them together and make jokes about their lovebirds. They would not hold hands in public, but their legs would touch under the table and he would place his bare feet on hers and they would smile in a foolish way. Then they would go back to the cave and make love, learning how to make the other happy. She asked,

Is it OK with you?

And he said it was and she was pleased.

They thought seriously about one another, for it became clear that their time together was not enough. This was not an ordinary relationship. It was difficult because of the distance and their different class and his dialect, but they were no longer two people. They were one person, their souls had merged, they saw the world through one pair of eyes. They just enjoyed being together, but Pablos was worried about Ioanna. He had the feeling that she was overwhelmed by her feelings, frightened of losing control. He was not good with words, but he opened up and in a simple way tried to tell her about his feelings.

I love you, he said. I want to be with you. I will do anything for this.

She was moved by his words and wanted to explain, but despite her sophistication all she could say was,

Me too.

Then one day things changed. She came to the beach and he wasn't there; the boat was pulled up out of the water and the cave was empty. The children ran to her, told her he was in his house, but to hurry. There she found him, pacing about, tired and grey and worried and angry. His mother was inside, a doctor was with her, and she was very, very ill. She had refused to take tablets that were given to her months before and now she was in pain. She had an infection, she was dying. He explained these things to Ioanna and they went inside to sit by the old woman. They sat holding hands through the night, and in the early morning as a wash of pale yellow spread from the horizon and softly lit the silent room, the old lady died. The women of the village, as was the custom, were waiting outside. When he told them she was dead, they wailed and keened and rent their clothes and took off their headscarves to let down their long, grey hair and scratched their faces until they bled. Ioanna and Pablos waited outside while the women came in to prepare his mother for her journey. They washed her and dressed her in clean clothes and wrapped her in clean sheets. They took away the old bedclothes to be burnt and sat by her bed and sang hymns and old songs of grief. They alerted the village carpenter to make a coffin. When it was were ready, the priest came and Pablos and the people of the village went in procession up the hill to the cemetery. Ioanna stayed behind and she could see the procession as it went by and she could see the silhouettes of the villagers and the black coffin held high against the sky. At the front she could recognise his shape, bible black and bent, as he stumbled and swayed while he held in his pain. From the far side of the hill she could hear the chapel bell, *ding-ding, ding-ding, ding-ding*.

When he returned from the hill, Ioanna asked

Are you OK?

And he said yes, but he was not.

For a while they continued as before. Ioanna loved him and cared for him and helped him with his mother's things. He felt strange, because he did not miss his mother, but over the weeks he grew angry inside and morose and Ioanna became nervous. He did not notice these things, for he was preoccupied deep within himself. He had discovered that he could not, did not want, no, could not make love. A psychiatrist, a skilled person, maybe an old person from the village, could explain what the problem was straight away. When someone close to you dies, for a while you avoid intimacy. But Pablos had no idea what was happening and neither did Ioanna and in folk stories there are fairy godmothers and glass slippers, but no psychiatrists. He loved Ioanna, but grief had taken his energy and he had no words to explain. A barrier came between them. They sat quietly at weekends while he drank, and at night she lay expectant by his side and waited for the love that he could not give. She was frightened and insecure, she wasn't confident enough to wait. Inside she panicked, she imagined problems. She asked why they no longer made love and he tried to explain that he could not, but she did not understand and she was not gentle with him. He withdrew into himself. Love and intimacy were so important to them and he was frightened of losing her. He knew that this would pass if he were left alone for a little while. He trusted Ioanna, but in her need she put pressure on him and, because he loved her and only because he loved her, he forced himself. One night he tried and it all went wrong and it was all a mistake and she shouted at him and called him names, bad, bad names

Our psychiatrist would say that she did not mean these things, she was only trying to get through to him, to break down the barrier that neither of them wanted nor understood. But Pablos did not understand what was happening as Ioanna shouted at him... He was so negative, he was mean, a shit, he didn't take her seriously, he was only a . . .

But she only meant to say fisherman, she only meant to say . . . she was not going to call him that. But he thought she was going to say it and she knew that was what he thought. She could not say sorry. She could not say anything. The cave was silent, deadly silent, and he turned slowly away, hurt and gutted like a freshly caught tuna. The roof was low and in the dark his head hit the rock and he fell to his knees as she ran from the cave and up the beach. She stumbled in the dark and took her bike and sped away, shocked by what had happened. The blood ran into his eyes . He too was shocked. He did not know what to do. Then, as he lay in the sand, the fear and panic subsided and he longed for his dead mother, and he understood and he cried.

The professor was quiet for a while, tired by all this storytelling, so I told him to wait and went inside to fetch more ouzo. He was sitting there in the dark when I returned.

Go on.

He paused, then,

Our fisherman was a self-critical and forgiving man and he told himself she could not help what she had done. He knew also that he could have done things differently and was ready to explain as he waited for her the next weekend. But she did not come. Nor did she come the weekend after that, nor the one after that. He was desolate. He did not know where she was; he did not know what to do. He could not understand how someone he loved could go away from him. The people of the village said many things; she was insecure, she was selfish, a fool, her father had abused her, she could not trust men. He should forget her.

Now he did not care about the weather, did not care about the storms. He would challenge the sea when it was rough and shout her name into the wind and taste the salt tears mixed with spray, as his little boat plunged and reared and rocked and shook. At night he sat alone in the cave and drank black rum. He drank till his liver hurt and, when he woke in the night, his body smelt rank and sour. Every day he looked up the beach for her bicycle, but it was never there. He had to do something, so, after a while, he went to the city to find her. It was strange to him and very big. He was sad as he looked through the lighted windows to find that all the flats were painted white and in none of them could he see Ioanna. He walked by the harbour and marvelled at the size of the ships and he walked in the park, with fallen leaves scuffling under his feet, as soft street lamps shimmered through a filter of rain. By a lake he saw lovers in cafes, drinking warm red wine and brandy, and heard happy voices as people cycled past. He felt warm inside to know that he was breathing the same air as Ioanna and to know that when the church bell rang she could hear it too. Then he heard the ferry boat's siren and he knew it was time to leave.

Many times he went to the city, but he could not find her, so he gave up, stayed in the village. Alone. The earth revolved and the moon came and went and the leaves on the trees did the same. He no longer loved life. He did not love the sea and he did not want to fish. There were no colours, birds did not sing. His heart was broken.

Then, somewhere, dice rolled.

Little Maxie, the smallest of the beach children, came back to the village. Her mother had moved to the city to work in the dock side bars and Maxie had gone with her, to go to school. She came breathless to his house. She stood there wide-eyed and beautiful, with long eyelashes and so grown up and so excited.

Pablos, Pablos, I seen Annie.
Who?
Annie
Ioanna? Her name sounded strange to his ears.
Yeah, Annie.

She told him that Ioanna taught at her new school and asked about him and wanted to know how he was.

He did not know what to do. He walked about, he got in his boat, he went out to sea. When he came back he walked up and down on the beach. Then he sat down with pencil and paper and tried to write. He scribbled and scribbled, he crossed out and scribbled again. He wanted to say so many things, but the words would not come. Then, somehow:

We lost our way. We can find it again.

He signed it H.

On Monday morning her hands shook, as she took the note from little Maxie. She did not want to hear from him, she did not want to know. It was over. Her feelings were buried, under control. Her life was lonely, but she was not going to allow herself to be hurt any more.

She read. She didn't like the note. She put it away. Read it again. Put it away.

Suddenly, without thinking, she laughed. H. He wasn't H he was P. She thought it very funny. H for hunchback. He could say it. They could say it. They could be honest. She laughed again. He had made her laugh. But she would not go to see him. It was too late. She would not know what to say. She had loved him, he was a good man, but it wouldn't work.

Time went by and she did nothing, but then one Saturday, without a plan, she found herself cycling to the beach. She smiled. She cried a little. She was doing the right thing. They would talk sensibly, they would discuss what had happened and if they had no feelings for one another it would not matter. She was strong enough.

But it was too late. He was gone.

She smelt the smoke first and then saw the glow of a bonfire on the beach. She saw a boat burning and nets. His boat. His nets.

The children ran to her, talking all at once. At first their thick accents disguised what they were saying.

There was a storm. He went out alone. He did not come back. The other fisherman went to look for him, to find him before the fish took his eyes. But they could not find him. They found the nets, they found the boat. It was full of water. So we waited for two weeks and now, we burn his things so that he will find them in heaven.

And then

He was a nice man. We liked him.

A cold wave ran through her body, she held her arms round her breasts.

Yes, a nice man. I liked him too.

She walked slowly to the cave. She was weak, she was cold. She took his blankets and wrapped herself in them and sat down. She could smell his body and feel his arms around her. The night came and the moon shone silver on the silent sea. On the horizon she could see the lights of fishing boats. She could not sleep. She did not cry. She was shocked. She was scared. She lay there and thought of their times together, the laughter, the affection, the love. Sometimes she heard her name, but it was only the wind.

Ioanna.

Ioanna.

Before dawn, when the horizon was a grey pencil line and the sun was not there, she stood up and slowly, very slowly, walked into the warm, enveloping sea.

In the morning, when the children came to the cave, it was empty.

But, children, being children did not believe she had gone. Sometimes they saw seals and sometimes at night they could hear the song of a seal and they thought it was not a seal, but a mermaid and the mermaid was Ioanna. And the story grew and it changed and was told in the bars and *cafeneion*s. The story of the hunchback who drowned and the woman who turned into a mermaid so she could search for him under the sea.

The professor was silent in the dark. He was tired. The sea breeze chilled the air. I suggest a cognac and went to fetch them. When I returned he was gone. I looked around. I thought I saw a crooked shadow play across the far side of the plaza, but nothing else moved. I sat and waited. I sipped the cognac thinking about what I had heard. It grew cold so I went inside to ask Gabriella where was the professor.

Professor? He's not a professor. He used to be a fisherman on the next island. He's got some kind of handicap. Comes here now and again and asks if we have seen any mermaids or some such nonsense.

My forehead feels damp. I shiver. I pay the bill and walk to my little house up the hill. The sea breeze is strong now, the Sirocco is coming and I hear waves pound the beach. I stand in my doorway, in the dark, listening to the sea. Is that something else I hear? A faint voice?

Ioanna

Ioanna.

Or just my imagination?

We have Commandos here

I was driving up from Pigadia to the village one day. Carefully, because it was raining and the road is not paved and it can be dangerous. I had covered some 10 kilometres and saw, a little way ahead, a woman from the village. She had a small bag over one shoulder, was dressed in village clothes and *stivania*, the old style boots, and she was running. I stopped the car and beckoned her in. We talked on the way to Olymbos.

Why are you running?

Because it's raining.

Where have you come from?

Pigadia.

Where are you going?

Olymbos.

She talked to me like I was an idiot. Of course you run if it's raining. And if it's more than forty kilometres and you are more than sixty years old, so what. You have to get home don't you? But she was interested in me. Was I Greek? How long had I lived in the village? And so on. We had a nice conversation but she used the thick Olymbos women's dialect and I found it hard going. I left her at the edge of her village, cackling away, and went down to mine. Sheltering in the *cafeneion*, out of the rain that night, I talked to her grandson over an ouzo. He was amused, but not surprised.

She's a tough woman. I said

We don't have women here we have commandos.

And it's true. The women here are very tough. The men too, but somehow the women are tougher and often bigger. They have hard lives.

If you sit on the veranda of *The Gorgona* restaurant, you have a wonderful view of the sea and the cliffs as far as the cape. It is best to sit there in the evening and watch the sea, mountains and sky change in the light. First the mountains are dark and the sea reflects the light from the sky. Then, as the sun goes, the mountains reflect the moon and shine out in three dimensions, as the sky and the sea darken. It is wonderful too to fish and dive around the cape and Georgos and I often go there. We were between there and Mavri Petra (Black Rock) one time and, as we got dried and dressed, Georgos pointed up the steep cliff and said there was a path there. I believed him, but could not see a way up these 200 metre cliffs. He told me a story.

He was twelve years old; his mother was around forty and needed to go to Tristomo with friends to gathe*r horta* for their goats. They only had a rowing boat, so Georgos was pressed into rowing them to the rocks at the foot of the path. Three large women, a heavy wooden boat, a twelve year-old boy and a ten kilometre round trip. They got there and Georgos watched them up the cliff, gossiping and laughing as they do. He fished a while with *katheti*, but the wind came and he knew he could not wait for them as planned, so he returned to the village. His mother would be fine; they had food and there was more to be gathered in Tristomo and there was shelter there in the old houses. But it was two days before the wind dropped and he could row back north again. He waited and waited, fishing a while, but nobody came. It was getting dark and, despite the fact that he was only wearing sayonaras (flip flops), he anchored the boat and off he went up the cliff to fetch the women. He got lost. It is rough on those mountains with scrub, thorns and thistles, and soon he was wandering around in the dark with shredded sayonaras, bleeding feet and no visible path. He whistled and shouted until his mother heard him, lit a fire to guide him and went to find her little boy. They spent their third night in Tristomo and returned all together the next day.

So what's so special about this story? Nothing. Absolutely nothing. In our village it is normal for young boys to take boats out in rough seas, though they normally have an outboard motor these days. It is normal, too, for women to climb cliffs and walk several kilometres to distant pastures to gather *horta*, or fruit, or olives. I know an old lady of over ninety who regularly goes to the north of Saria with her family to milk goats and make cheese. The tourists have no idea and the men sitting in the *cafeneion* do not bother to comment. It is nothing special.

And Georgos' mother, Marina? She is over seventy now and a big, powerful woman, built, as she says, like Mavri Petra itself. She walks four or more kilometres every evening to milk her goats and back again. She goes through the forest where the fire was years ago. She reports on useful fallen trees and recently we all went there to gather a large one. With adze, chain and hand saw we cleared a space, cut the trunk into three sections and began to move the large logs down the hillside. Georgos' mother was feeding her goats, but keeping an eye on us. I am a big man, fit and strong, but it wasn't easy rolling a 110 kg log end over end across the rough terrain. I paused for breath, lifted up one end and suddenly she was there, lifting the other end of the log, placing it on her shoulder and off she went dragging me, shouting and slipping behind, with Georgos' laughter following us down the gully. I shouted at her to stop, as I struggled along to keep up, trying not to drop my end of the log. She just laughed and when we reached the road to the village she threw the log aside and turned to me with a triumphant look. She had made her point., She, an old woman, was stronger than me.

But it's not just the women. Last summer, one afternoon I was out there, off the cape, fishing for my supper. The sea was calm, but I was surprised to see, coming from the north, somebody rowing along on their way to the village. It was Iannis in his wooden boat with the outboard motor out of the water. Now I like Iannis, he is a lovely man and I respect him a great deal. He lives with his wife in Tristomo, the other side of the island. They have a simple life there with their goats and their cheese and fish and the wild fruit and vegetables. I took in my line and motored over to see what was the problem and if I could help.

Do you have a problem?

No.

Have you run out of petrol? A not uncommon occurrence.

No.

Do you want me to tow you to the village?

No.

How will you get there?

With my oars.

Now, it's rather strange to meet someone out at sea and to have a conversation with them like they are going to fetch the newspapers, but, if he didn't want any help, there was nothing I could do. So I left him there, standing up, facing the way he was going and leaning with his body into his oars with an action that looks so strange to scullers, but which is very efficient.

We met a couple of days later in the village. We shook hands; he has a very strong grip and it hurt. I asked him what had been the problem.

The engine was broke, he said, and he was fetching it to be fixed.

Where did it break? Thinking up the coast a way.

Tristomo. Now Tristomo is 12 kilometres away by sea.

You rowed from Tristomo?

Yes. How else was I to get here?

And he strode away, no doubt thinking he had enough of these daft questions from an ignorant foreigner. Oh, by the way, Iannis is 65 years old.

Some time ago you could see a man in the village with one arm. His name was Costas. He had been brought up in the time when the Italians were here and spoke Italian as well as Greek. He liked to talk to tourists, but nobody asked him about his arm. Here is the story. After the war there were no fishing nets here. They had all been confiscated by the Germans and the men learnt to use explosives to fish. He lost his arm while fishing, not with dynamite but with a bomb made from a bottle of petrol, some wax and a rag round the top. Something went wrong, there was a premature explosion and Costas was left alone in a boat with his right arm in tatters. When he became conscious his arm was bleeding badly so he took a rope and made a tourniquet. He was off the coast near a beach called Papa Minas, some half an hour south of the village. Costas tried to start the engine. It would not start. He tried again. Nothing. So with one arm, in great pain and still bleeding heavily, he opened the engine to look inside. He took out the spark plugs. He cleaned them. Put them back in. Tried to start the engine. It started. Praying all the while, and gritting his teeth against the shock and the pain, Costas made it back to the village. He ran his boat up the beach and shouted and screamed. The villagers came, carried him out of the boat and took him to hospital. He lost his arm, but he lived.

Commandos. All of them are commandos.

The Story of the Cave

The people of the village walk slowly, with a rhythm accustomed to distant places and long journeys by foot, carrying heavy loads. It is a graceful walk, unhurried and calm. There is one exception. His name is Vasillis Balaskas. He darts around like a demented wagtail; a pause here, a move there, stop at the *cafeneion*, shift to the end of the harbour, pause at Michalis', say hello to Gabriella, back to the Golden Beach. As a young man in the village he was the captain of an old wooden *caique*, carrying freight and people around the islands, sometimes as far as Piraeus. Quite a trip for a small *caique* and a twenty-two year old captain. Quite a responsibility and a very busy life. Then, like so many others, Vasillis went to America. There he worked hard, created his own construction company and saved money. Life in New York thirty years ago was not that easy for an uneducated Greek, but Vasillis clawed his way up and eventually got enough money together to return to the village and build a hotel. It is a good hotel, in the valley on the way to Olympos, quiet and clean and friendly.

Inevitably Vasillis will come close to talk to you. He has a weather-beaten face, brown and wrinkled. His eyes are alive, he is alert and calculating, elegant too with fashionable clothes and Rayban sunglasses. He looks a hard man;

you wouldn't want to mess with him. But don't be fooled, he is soft too and kind, and he laughs a lot.

But this story is not about Vasillis, it is about his genes.

In the early nineteenth century northern Karpathos was a wild place, but wilder still was Saria. The rule of law did not extend that far; the inhabitants did not pay taxes and no police ever set foot on the island. Much in fact like today. There were olive groves and terraces and fig trees and beehives. Farmers lived there for part of the year in simple *stavlos* (one storey houses), returning to Olymbos, Avlona or Tristomo from time to time. Shepherds lived there too, but, as they moved around looking for fresh pasture for their sheep and goats, they lived in caves or slept overnight in simple stone constructions a metre or two high.

One such shepherd was Iannis. His main habitation was a large cave on the way to Palatia. You can see it from the sea and in the old days there was a difficult path up from the bay below. Iannis lived there, from time to time, with his wife. One day a *caique* appeared and anchored in the bay below the cave. Nine men disembarked, Syrians or Turks, it does not matter which. In the old language they would have been called *Arabis*. Their occupation? Piracy. Their target? The plump sheep around the cave. His wife shouted at him to do something, but Iannis could not do much about nine men. He could have thrown rocks down on them, but they were armed with muskets and would have shot him. He could have run away, but a good shepherd does not abandon his flock, or his wife. To raise the alarm in those days you blew into a large, spiral conch shell that let out the sound of a trumpet. We still have these shells and we call them *trambouki*, and a loud-mouthed person is called *tramboukas*. Iannis sounded the alarm, but nobody came. The men arrived at the cave. Iannis tried to appear friendly. They made him kill a sheep and roast it. They helped themselves to wine. They ate his sheep and drank the wine and all the while made threats and behaved the way that pirates and brigands are supposed to behave. They told him to make *misithra*. This is a soft, creamy, cheese made from sheep's milk. You make it by boiling milk in a large cauldron and stirring it with a big wooden spoon for hour after hour.

Iannis kept calm. He tried to befriend the pirates. He made *misithra* and, as he stirred the hot milk, he thought. He found some more wine. The *Arabis* drank it. Full stomachs, a hot day, wine, a smoke-filled cave and soon the men were dozing off. Iannis carried on stirring the boiling milk. He waited, he stirred, he waited. He put cloths on his hands. He looked at his wife. He lifted the cauldron of scalding milk, walked quietly to the first sleeping brigand and poured milk over his head and the next and the next and the next. There were screams, mayhem and the next and the next. He scalded and blinded eight of the men. They ran around blindly inside the cave in pain and agony. The ninth escaped and ran down the hill. Iannis and his wife took clubs and knives and killed the blinded pirates. They were both strong people and killing comes naturally if your profession is a shepherd and your life is threatened. When the killing was finished in the cave Iannis took up a musket went outside, tracked the ninth man and shot him.

It was quiet in the cave. Iannis and his wife sat awhile in the late afternoon sun. They talked. They took the bodies outside and buried them in the nearby olive grove. They cleaned the cave. They continued their life. A heroic couple on a heroic, savage, island.

Is the story true? To be sure there is a resonance with myths and stories from ancient Greek times — caves, shepherds, blinded men, perhaps the cyclops. I am told that it is true and that if you look in the olive grove you will find the bones of nine men. One day I will go and look.

Who told me this story? Michalis, a charming and lively old man of 88 years who builds footpaths and thinks nothing of walking 20 kilometres or more to Olymbos and Avlona when he is bored. Michalis lived in America, yet speaks no English. With his arms waving and eyes sparkling he sits in the *cafeneion* and brings it all alive with ancient curses from the time of Alexander. Lions and eagles, he shouts and describes the *Arabis* as big and black, *Palikaria*, with white teeth and rings on their fingers and guns over their shoulders. He tells me the shepherd was his great, great, great grandfather, and I believe him.

Who is this Michalis?

He is Michalis Balaskas, the father of Vasillis. You remember him, a soft and kind man who laughs a lot.

If you don't steal his sheep, that is.

The Big Fish

For many years I resisted the pressure to take up diving. The pressure came from Georgos, the best diver on this part of the island. By diving I mean wearing mask, fins, flippers and wet suit and diving under the sea with a harpoon gun to hunt fish. It is forbidden to use compressed air to hunt fish in Greece. We dive without air. I resisted because it is tiring and dangerous. I have enough to do in this village and I could never have enough breath to go down to the depths that Georgos reaches. He has been down to 30 metres and can hold his breath for two minutes and he can do this for hour after hour.

Then one day I tried it. I took my boat to a quiet beach where the sea is shallow and where there are plenty of rocks. I put on mask and flippers and, with a borrowed gun, began splashing around. I saw what seemed to be a big fish and became hooked. The fish did not. Nor was it harpooned and as far as I know it never has been, but I knew that diving was one thing I had to do. So, slowly, slowly, I learnt how to do it, how to anchor my boat off a beach, how to put on the suit and the flippers and weights and mask. I learnt about safety; always have a balloon to show the many short-sighted fishermen and boat owners around here where you are diving. I learnt how to get into the sea without getting tied up in the various lines and ropes that surround fishing and I learnt how to dive under the water. Most importantly I learnt how to get back into the boat. This is not an easy operation.

The physics of diving do not require that you swim down; on the contrary, you swim up. Your wet suit is buoyant; in the sea, it holds you up. You wear a belt of weights to neutralise this buoyancy so that, when horizontal, you can swim along the surface. When you tilt to the vertical (not an easy trick) the surface area you present to the sea is less and you have less buoyancy. The weights take you down. After about four metres there is sufficient water pressure above and your lungs are compressed sufficiently that you are pushed deeper and, unless you flatten out, you will keep going down. To come up you have to swim. You look up at the underside of the sea, silver and far above, and you kick slowly and gently, close to panic as you desperately hold your breath for those last few seconds. Going down, your lungs are squeezed smaller and smaller until they are the size of mandarin oranges. Going down, you hold your nose to equalise the pressure inside your ears to that of the water outside, so that your eardrums are not ruptured. Going down, you prepare to look under rocks, go into caves, shoot a fish. These are dark experiences. Coming up, you head towards light and air, the joy of breath, the feeling of rebirth. The certainty of life.

Diving is good exercise. You develop flexibility, good breath control, a slow pulse and mental awareness. It is like yoga, with the additional advantage that, if you are any good, you get to eat fresh fish. I know enough now to go out on my own and shoot around one kilo of fish an hour. That is enough for supper for myself and for company. I do this and I also dive with Georgos. This is to be in the presence of a maestro. We proceed parallel to the coast, me close to the shore, Georgos further out. We separate, meet again, separate and come back together. We are aware of the dangers. I like to watch Georgos, but it is scary. Down he goes, 20, 25, 30 metres. It is dark blue to black down there and he often disappears into caves. All I can see is the line going in from his marker balloon and the occasional escape of bubbles of air. Down there, if there is a problem — and you can get stuck in caves — there is nothing that I could do to help. Sometimes, when either of us finds a big fish, we act as a team. Georgos will dive to shoot the fish and then we work together to bring it to the surface. If it is a grouper it will be in a hole slightly larger than itself and it cannot just be pulled out. Often, even if the fish is shot, it will not be dead and pulling on the harpoon does not work. You can break the harpoon, or damage the fish or cut your hands on the sharp gills and spines of the fish. A twenty-kilo grouper is the size of a full-grown Alsatian dog, but stronger and with more and sharper teeth. They go back in rows all the way down its throat. A grouper is an eating machine and if your hand went in there it would not come out. So getting a big grouper out of its lair is not easy. Sometimes we use a plastic *pagouri* or container (my boat is full of them) about one gallon in size. Georgos ties a line to the *pagouri* and dives down to attach it to the harpoon, which of course is buried in the fish. It is very strange to see him sitting there, carefully tying a knot, 20 metres, or more, under the sea. He signals and I dive a little way pulling the *pagouri* under the water. Another signal and I release it gently. As it floats towards the surface there is a constant, but gentle pressure on the fish and after a while the fish comes out and we have supper. Or if it's a big fish we have some money. In this way we have caught fish of twenty kilos and more, and they are very valuable.

Is shooting fish cruel? Yes, it must be, but I promised myself when I started on this journey, that, if I was going to eat it, I was going to kill it. So far I have killed fish, chicken and goats. Being a carnivore is not always pleasant. I do not like killing octopus. They are smart creatures, as smart as a cat for example, and use any trick they can to escape capture, but I like to eat octopus. One time I dived down too steep and hit the bottom. As I did so I saw a strange pair of eyes rise up the other side of a rock. As I bounced back to the surface these eyes lowered. The same thing happened again. Up, down, up, down. It was an octopus with eyes in the top of its body watching me, a Walt Disney creation making me laugh under the sea. I didn't kill it. But I should have done.

On the surface of the sea, when in my boat, I have seen many incredible and beautiful things: turtles migrating to lay their eggs on some distant beach, manta rays, big fish, seals and dolphins. The encounter with the manta rays was the most weird. These are huge creatures, about the size of my boat. They weigh around half a ton and look fearsome, but are harmless plankton eaters. We were fishing with a line for small fish one day in a sea that was without wind, but with a heavy and persistent swell. And there they were. As we went down into a trough we could see three great, dark shapes rise above us in a wave. We rose again and looked down on the mantas gently flowing on with a soft movement, gliding through the ocean. When you see wild creatures close up, especially strange, large, wild creatures, your feelings are confused — awe, fear, excitement, fear again and an inner feeling of calm and reverence and perhaps privilege. We stood up, pointing and laughing, shouting to one another. Look, look three of them. And then came the fourth. Was it bigger than the others? It seemed darker too. It seemed to notice us standing up and turned and headed towards us to check us out. Manta rays have eyes on the end of twin stalks and, as it came close, these swivelled towards us and we looked at one another from maybe three metres. The creature was clearly less impressed with us than we were with it and slowly it turned away to join its compatriots. In my little boat it was silent. We had been in the presence of something formidable.

There have been many encounters with dolphins. They enter our nets, steal our fish and leave great holes, which Georgos spends hours fixing with care and precision, cursing the dratted creatures, but without anger or sincerity. We have seen them leaping and spinning, doing back flips and somersaults, presumably for fun. One time, when the sea was boiling with tuna fish and shearwaters were diving into this heaving mass, we saw large dolphins tearing through the shoal, like wartime destroyers, in a frantic frenzy of feeding. On another quiet night we came across a circle of little dolphins in the harbour. Round and round they went, head to tail, a few metres from the shore, with its restaurants and tourists and lights, having fun in their own unfathomable way. But my favourite encounter was when alone, far out in a dead calm but misty sea, I saw a long black rope floating on the surface. I went carefully in that direction. The rope disappeared and appeared again 10 metres further on. The same thing happened, and again. But now I noticed that the surface of the sea was oily where the rope had been and I felt a little unsure. A whale perhaps, or shark? Something big anyway. And then the rope appeared again, closer this time and I could see that it was moving slowly along and that my rope consisted of four or five large dolphins each with its nose resting on the tail of the one in front. Only the last one was swimming with a slow tail movement that propelled these sleek creatures gently along. Can you say that dolphins are lazy, or that they have a sense of humour? I don't know, but I am a trained scientist and observer and I felt that they were playing games with me.

Under the sea it is different. This is an alien environment. The colours can be astounding and the creatures, big and small, abundant, but I don't belong there. For tens of seconds, a minute at the most, I can catch a glimpse of this world at eight, nine or ten metres. I can observe, watch, wait and, if lucky, will see a fish big enough to shoot. And, if luckier still, will shoot it, hastily return to the surface, thread the fish onto my line and plan the next move. Sometimes an octopus, sometimes a sea bream or *sargoss*, as they call them here, rarely a grouper, more often than not a *scarros*, the staple fish of the island that the old people turn into tasty casserole. Occasionally, at a distance, you see a big fish, but until this particular day the biggest I had seen was around fifteen kilograms.

We were diving off the north west of Saria, a fascinating place with steep underwater cliffs. There I floated, looking down at layers of deeper and deeper blue, as shoals of fish hung suspended with me, drifting past, turning slowly in the current, moving up and down with the waves. In some places it is impossible to see the bottom and that gives an unreal feeling of solitude. Like being lost in space, you could fall forever. Elsewhere there are caves and rocks and here I can look for fish and even lobsters. Georgos was about ten metres ahead of me, checking each hole and cave in his slow, methodical way. I followed, erratic, uncouth, without grace or balance and then saw, a few metres below, the entrance to a large cave. Three deep breaths and I was down there, peering in, and suddenly I was face to face with the biggest fish I have seen in all my life. A grouper, more than 20 or 22 kilograms. I could have reached out and touched it. I could have shot it with my harpoon. I would have hit it for sure, but my spear gun would not have killed it and I knew that it would go deeper into the cave, maybe to die from its injuries. It is a sin to damage such a wonderful creature, so I watched in awe as it slowly, carefully turned away and, with a petulant flick of its tail reached the back of the cave, maybe ten metres away, and disappeared into its hole.

Georgos, Georgos, Georgos. *Ella dw*, over here. And he came and I explained and showed him where it had gone. One minute before he had checked the cave and seen nothing. Probably out of curiosity, the grouper had come out to check him and found me. Excitedly I explained what I had seen, how we could catch the fish, what I thought would be the next move. But Georgos would have none of it. The weather had changed. It was late and we had to go.

Back in the boat we prepared to leave. Georgos was thoughtful.

Now we must dance a little.

And he was right, though not at first. We could keep in close to the rocks and out of the storm, but later, as we reached the southwest corner of Saria, the full force of the sea was upon us. We could not turn eastwards along the channel, we were too close to dangerous rocks for that, and, if the sea came sideways towards us, water would come into the boat. So I steered directly into the wind, directly into the waves. These were three metres high now and to get anywhere you accelerate as you go up the wave and slow down as you go down into the trough again. This is worrying and tiring and we had to go several kilometres out to sea before we could safely turn. Meanwhile Georgos was calmly fishing with a hand line with thirteen hooks and, every now and again pulling in the line. To be cold, wet, tired and a little frightened is one thing. To head into a force seven storm in a four point three metre boat with a ten horse-power engine is bearable. But to have lines, hooks, blood, shit and live tuna fish sloshing around your bare feet seemed a little too complicated. I explained this to Georgos in Greek fisherman's language and, after a two minute stand up shouting match, he conceded, pulled in the line and busied himself sorting out our fish. Anything that stops Georgos fishing must be serious, so I concentrated even harder as we slid up and plummeted down dark grey waves under the silver sky. Eventually it was safe to turn sideways at the top of a wave and then, with a powerful sea behind us, to go surfing back towards Saria. It took an hour to make two kilometres along the coast, but we were finally safe within the lee of Karpathos.

By the time we got back to the village it was dark and there were one or two worried faces. They had seen us set off and had seen the weather change dramatically. Something that, being under the sea, we had not noticed. That night as we ate prime fish we were a little subdued. Not only by the weather, but also by the big fish. Of course, we spoke of neither. The time was November and it was the last dive of the year. Next year we will go back. That is a good fish and a valuable fish. It will be a little dangerous diving into such a deep cave, but working together we should manage.

Meanwhile, in some cafe, or standing in a bar drinking with friends, I think of the fish. I know it is safe. I know where it is and, more or less, what it is doing. Suddenly I do not belong in the neon-lit, shrill, twenty-first century. I belong in a different time at a different place. I should be there, in the cold and the dark, under the sea, hunting the big fish. I try to return to the conversation, but I cannot. I give up and go home early.

Strange guy, they say. Wonder what he was thinking about?

Diaspora

Throughout Europe, especially on the fringes, there has been a tremendous movement of people, to towns and cities, to other countries, other continents. For fifty years and more this movement has been relentless. Peoples moving, hearts breaking, communities breaking up. The west of Ireland, for example saw the young girls moving to Dublin and then to America to work in bars and hotels and to skivvy for the rich. The men, left behind, formed communities of bachelors, drinking heavily in bars in the summer, when there were tourists and life, and staring into their pints of Guinness in the winter, when there were none.

With this village it was Baltimore and New York and Canada, especially the far north, but above all Baltimore. There are three hundred families from our village living there now. The old women still wear their traditional clothes as daily wear and the blacks and the Irish and the street kids don't know the difference between them and Muslims from Arabia or Pakistan. The young men still play our music, the young girls wear the clothes and dance on feast days and holidays, marriages are still arranged and home is still our village. Each family has a house here, or land anyway. They return every summer, or Easter, or every ten years. But if they can, they return.

The exodus started early here. One young man went to Baltimore and after a few years sent for his family. Why Baltimore? Nobody knows. Years ago I sat with an old man of eighty-four outside his house in a village not far from here, on the first night of his return from America. He had come back home to leave his bones in their proper place. He cried as he told me his story, but he was not ashamed. He had left his village in 1915 for America, travelled to Athens by *caique* and then steerage class by steamer, ten days across the Atlantic. He worked hard on building sites, a master of cement. Then, still a young man, he came back for a wife, picked out for him by his mother. They returned to America, where there were already others from the village, had children, lived their life. Now he was back for the first time since 1926, sitting in his yard, in the dark, with a stranger, crying to see his home again, to hear the voices, to see the sea.

Those that went could not, of course write back and say how terrible life was. Instead they told of riches, of cars, big houses and plenty of food. So that when they returned there were women waiting to marry them and, when they left again, they took their young brides with them. And so it continues today. Young men leave, work hard, save money, come back to find a bride and off they go again. They work in bars and in tavernas, they drive taxis, fit aluminium cladding to terraced houses, they run their own businesses, own restaurants. I even know, and this is absolutely true, of one man who has been to the North Pole, to the scientific base there as a heating engineer! He looked in the guest book. There were no Greek names there. The first Greek at the North Pole. From our village. He has been there three times and now he sits in Anna's, sometimes telling stories, sometimes asleep.

If they don't come back, or if they do and are loud and brash, we say, 'Too much Coca Cola', and we don't care when they leave again. The best come back and stay. They stay because they like our village, the community, the weather, our language and our sense of humour. They come back because they know that we have something better, more valuable than dollars, more lasting than big cars and loud music. They bring their money with them, buy fridges and televisions, rebuild family houses and sit in the *cafeneion* playing *tavli* and listening to the old men.

The hardest times were in the war. Not when the Italians were here, but after, when the Germans came in 1944. Then the people starved and the women and children walked all over the mountains looking for snails, edible roots, plants and flowers. The men that were left picked limpets and cockles from the rocks and fished when the Germans let them and sometimes when they did not. The war did not end in '45. It continued in civil war and then repression, so that families left to find freedom and democracy as well as work and money.

Through all this, the village people have kept their customs, their language, their traditions. They have kept family ties, so that each one knows of first, second and sometimes third cousins from over there that they have never met. The people commute between here and Baltimore; summer at home, winter in America. When the children go to college, whole families decamp to be with them in Piraeus, or Athens, or Rhodes. And, as they get more money, young people stay here over the winter, determined that the community will not die. There are more children in the schools than twenty years ago, more people living in the village than then. We have emails, hi fi's, an internet cafe.

If we work in the fields, growing our own wheat and rye, if we fish when others tie up their boats and shelter in the taverna, that's our choice. We live the way we want. Do you? When you walk around our village with your video camera and your instant this and digital that, trying to capture, in a few minutes, the soul of the village, do you think of these things? Or are you living in a world created by brochures and smart salesmen; a world that tells of simple people living in a timeless, unspoilt, landscape? When you see these old men do you know that they have lived in Canada, or Poland or the USA? When you scurry to photograph the old lady in the little house by the oven, the one with the striking features, do you know that she winters in New York and loves its buzz and excitement? Do you think of these things or not? If you think our food is strange, our customs are quaint, our clothes are weird, have you looked at yourself? Are we caricatures? Or is it you?

The *Cafeneion*

Closed now, not yet open for the summer season, but closed. Clean and shiny, smelling of polish and faded herbs. Empty, but somewhere, somehow, a voice, a clink of coins. Cards slap a table. Can you hear laughter, soft, as if far away? Are there memories here? Memories of friendly summers and snug, communal winters? Can you smell the ouzo? Can you taste it? Does the cap from a cold beer clatter on that marble counter? Where are the men with their rough jackets, their squeaky boots, their soft, mannered voices? The women, where are they, with dark eyes, black shawls, their shoes clipping across this hard wooden floor? Clip, clip, clip. Gone away, every one. Far, far away, for money, for children . . . for a better life.

What's left is a dark, empty room and a foolish old man looking through the window, wondering about the old days and the days that are to come.

Printed in the United Kingdom
by Lightning Source UK Ltd.
108893UKS00001B/183